*Puffin Books*
# No Gun For Asmir

'Asmir wondered when he would wake up in his own bed. Would the nightmare end soon? If only Muris would reach out and put his arm around him again. Then he heard Muris saying, "War never does make sense." And he knew he would not wake up in his own bed again. Ever.'

War has come to Asmir's home in Sarajevo. Asmir has seen his friends wounded, in the park where they used to play. He hears bombs exploding, guns firing, his parents talking in worried voices.

And then one morning he is torn from his father, his home and everything he has known. He becomes a refugee . . .

*A Children's Book Council of Australia Notable Book, 1994.*

*Highly Commended in the 1994 Human Rights Awards category of Literature and Other Writing – Children's Literature.*

## By the same author

# No Gun for Asmir

Christobel Mattingley
*Illustrated by Elizabeth Honey*

PUFFIN BOOKS

Puffin Books
Penguin Books Australia Ltd
487 Maroondah Highway, PO Box 257
Ringwood, Victoria 3134, Australia
Penguin Books Ltd
Harmondsworth, Middlesex, England
Viking Penguin, A Division of Penguin Books USA Inc.
375 Hudson Street, New York, New York 10014, USA
Penguin Books Canada Limited
10 Alcorn Avenue, Toronto, Ontario, Canada M4V 3B2
Penguin Books (N.Z.) Ltd
182–190 Wairau Road, Auckland 10, New Zealand

First published by Penguin Books Australia, 1993
10 9 8 7 6
Copyright © Christobel Mattingley, 1993
Illustrations Copyright © Elizabeth Honey, 1993

Typeset in 13½/15½pt Goudy Old Style by Midland Typesetters, Maryborough, Victoria
Made and printed in Australia by Australian Print Group, Maryborough, Victoria

National Library of Australia
Cataloguing-in-Publication data:

Mattingley, Christobel, 1931–
No gun for Asmir.

ISBN 0 14 036729 2.

I. Title

A823.3

All royalties from sales of this book go towards Asmir's education.

*For refugee families everywhere, especially Asmir's and others from Bosnia, and for the fathers who could not leave, especially Muris.*

# Contents

# Author's Note

This is a true story. The characters are real people. Because I was not with them when they escaped, I have used my imagination and my own experiences of former Yugoslavia, Hungary and Austria for some details and incidents. The families agreed to my telling their story in the hope it will help people understand. They have read it and approve.

On 6 April 1993, Melita said, 'That we are alive and here in Vienna is a miracle. That Muris and his mother are alive in Sarajevo is a miracle.

'Because this book will touch people and come to the heart, if only a hundred people read it and are moved, it will be more important than any official peace plan.'

# SARAJEVO TO VIENNA

Border of former
Yugoslavia ▬▬▬▬

Mirsada, Grandmother,
Asmir and Eldar's
route ▬ ▬ ▬ ▬

Milan's route ▬▬▬▬

Former
Yugoslavia

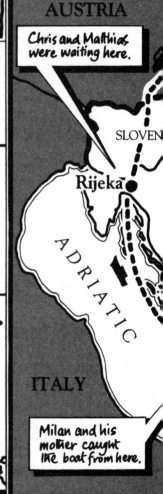

AUSTRIA

Chris and Matthias
were waiting here.

SLOVEN

Rijeka

ADRIATIC

ITALY

Milan and his
mother caught
the boat from here.

Pronounce the names this way:

| | |
|---|---|
| Asmir, *son of Muris and Mirsada* | **Azmeer** |
| Eldar, *Asmir's little brother* | **Eldar** |
| Mirsada, *Asmir's mother* | **Meersarda** |
| Dada, *Mirsada's pet name* | **Dardar** |
| Muris, *Asmir's father* | **Mooris** |
| | |
| Melita, *Asmir's aunt* | **Melleeta** |
| Miroslav, *Asmir's uncle* | **Mirroslarv** |
| | |
| Milan, *father of George* | **Millarn** |
| Vesna, *George's mother* | **Vezna** |
| George, *son of Milan and Vesna* | **Jorj** |
| | |
| Matthias, *Austrian* | **Matteeus** |
| Chris, *Australian* | **Kris** |
| | |
| Sarajevo, *capital of Bosnia Herzegovina* | **Sarryaivo** |
| Rijeka, *port of Croatia* | **Reeyaika** |

There are four grandmothers in the story:

Grandmother of Asmir and Eldar, *mother of Mirsada and Melita*
Grandmother of George, *mother of Milan*

Grandmother of Asmir and Eldar, *mother of Muris*
Grandmother of George, *mother of Vesna*

▲ Grandmother,
Mirsada, the
author and Asmir
in Chris's kitchen.

▶ Miroslav and
Melita with Eldar
meet Chris's
parents in Vienna.

▼ Muris

# 1  Sarajevo

Asmir comes from Bosnia Herzegovina. That name twists the tongues of people who do not know it. But Asmir was born in Sarajevo. And it rolls off his tongue like the smooth creamy sauce and the tender tasty meat of his grandmother's *musaka*.

Asmir remembers how the mountains rose sparkling with snow in the winter all around Sarajevo. And in the summer the trees swept like green waves up the slopes. The domed roofs of the mosques gleamed like moons among the houses and the minarets spiked the skyline. Morning, noon and evening the *muezzins'* call to prayer used to echo out across the city.

Asmir's father, Muris, was a lawyer in Sarajevo. Asmir's mother, Mirsada, was a chemical engineer in a chocolate factory. Asmir's brother Eldar was still only a baby, just twelve months old.

1

But Asmir had many other playmates. They used to meet each day in the park near their homes, running among the trees, chasing, hiding, swinging, see-sawing, rolling on the grass, calling, laughing.

Until one day, war came to Sarajevo. Hundreds of soldiers arrived, firing rifles, firing guns. Tanks rumbled through the streets. Aircraft flew over the city dropping bombs.

The smell of burning made Asmir's stomach sick. The smoke made his eyes sting. The sight of his friend the postman lying on the street with all the letters spilling out of his bag made his heart shudder. It was too late to help the postman.

Asmir gathered up the bloodstained letters. But when he took them to some of the addresses, the houses were burning heaps or hollow holes. He ran home clutching the crumpled envelopes. His grandmother washed his hands and cooked him *ustipci*. They were his very favourite. But that day he could not swallow. The pancakes stuck in his throat.

Morning and night the tanks rumbled and the rockets exploded. Midday the sky filled with droning planes and the crack of snipers' rifles. There was no electricity to amplify the *muezzins'* call. It seemed to Asmir as if the soldiers had bombed God.

Then they bombed the chocolate factory. The smell of the chocolate choked Asmir to the bottom of his lungs and made his stomach churn. The chocolate burned but his mother came home. Asmir hugged her tight, and that night he crept into bed between her and his father. And the bad dreams went away.

Day after day, night after night, week after week the war went on. Grandmother came to live with them because her apartment was gone. Meat became a treat, eggs were as scarce as hens' teeth. Of course there was no chocolate. And no ice-cream or lemonade either. Then there was no milk.

The daffodils were dancing in the park. The cherry trees were frothing white like the milk Asmir's father had loved on top of his coffee. But the playground had become a bomb crater and a cemetery. Two of Asmir's friends had been killed there. Another was in hospital. He would walk again only if he was given an artificial leg.

'Mirsada, there are no medicines left in the hospitals and no pain-killing drugs. You must go somewhere safe with the children,' Muris said to Asmir's mother. 'It's time for you to leave while you can. They're still letting women and children go. But tonight could be the last time they do.'

Asmir saw his mother's face go pale and

watched her dark eyes grow even darker. They looked like black holes of emptiness. She gripped her husband's hands. 'But Eldar has a fever. Can't we go tomorrow when he is better?'

'It's still safer in Serbia. You must go to your sister Melita in Belgrade,' Muris said. Asmir loved his aunt Melita.

His father said to him, 'Pack your holiday rucksack with your favourite toys and some for Eldar too. And help your mother choose some clothes. You can't take everything.'

Asmir put in their teddies, his best Lego and a bag of little farm animals, Eldar's cart and horse on wheels, a boat for the bath, some books, his coloured pencils and drawing pad. His mother crammed T-shirts, jeans, shorts, pyjamas, shoes and socks into a case.

Eldar was so restless that his mother slept beside him that night. So Asmir slept with his father. It was good to snuggle up with him. 'Why do we have to go away?' he asked. 'I don't want to leave you. Can't you come with us?'

'I wish I could,' his father said. 'But the war is getting worse every day. Yugoslavia has broken up. Serbia wants to take over Bosnia. That's why their army has invaded us.'

Invade. It was a crushing word. Asmir felt pinned down by it. As his friend had been by the falling wall.

4

His father went on. 'And women and children must have first chance to escape.'

Escape. A scary, running word. Almost worse than invade. His friend whose leg had been torn off by shrapnel couldn't run. He couldn't even walk. He couldn't escape.

'Why do we have to escape? Who are we escaping from?' Asmir's voice came out as a whisper in the dark.

'We're Muslim, Asmir. And *they* want to clean us out.'

'But we're clean already,' Asmir said, thinking of the washing dancing on the line, the gleaming copper cooking pots his grandmother loved to scour, the shining tiled floor, the crisp fresh clothes he put on each day. He stroked the smooth soft sheet. It was as soft as his grandmother's cheeks. And nobody could be cleaner than she was. 'Why do they want to clean us out? They're going about it in a very messy stupid way.'

He thought of the shattered glass, the piles of rubble, the splintered doors and sagging beams of houses in their own street, the proud trees in the playground blasted, split, stripped of their dancing leaves, dying.

'Who are *they*, anyway?'

His father groaned with a sigh that seemed to come from somewhere deeper than the graves

Asmir had seen men digging in his park, even deeper than the bomb crater. 'Lots of them were our friends, Asmir. Some of them were our neighbours. Your mother and I went to school and university with some of them. Your grandmothers played with their parents.'

'Then why are they fighting? It doesn't make sense.'

'War never does make sense,' Asmir's father said sadly. Asmir shivered and snuggled closer to him.

'Innocent people get hurt. Coming home from work one day your mother and I were caught between gunfire from both sides. We worry what would happen to you and Eldar if we were hurt.'

Asmir shuddered and tried to blot out the picture of the postman from his mind – so still, so crumpled. So bloody. 'Will they make you fight and kill people too?' The words stuck in his throat. Like the pancakes had.

'They'll make some people. But I don't want to kill anyone, Asmir. I'll volunteer to work in the hospital. They'll need every pair of hands they can get to care for the wounded.'

'I wish I could stay and help you,' Asmir said.

'You have a job to do too,' his father said. 'You'll have to look after your mother and Eldar and Grandmother now.'

'When will we come back?'

'I don't know. I only wish I did.'

Asmir suddenly felt old. Old and heavy. And very tired. His father put his arms around him. And that was all that mattered now. He fell asleep on his father's shoulder.

When he woke, the sunbeams were shimmering with dancing dust. Asmir coughed. There was always dust now from the bombing. He shivered. The bed was cold. He turned over. The bed was empty. 'Daddy,' he called. But there was no answer. Muris was gone.

## 2 Escape

Asmir ran to his own room. His mother was sponging Eldar who was still flushed and grizzly. She told Asmir to put on two of everything. He felt like a penguin waddling with its egg. 'Where's Daddy?'

'He's gone to work.'

Asmir thought of the snipers hiding in the ruined buildings, picking off people as they passed. Not Muris. Not Muris. He had to reach the office safely. Perhaps he would telephone in a few moments to let them know he was there.

His mother was dressing Eldar. 'I can do that,' Asmir offered. 'You'll be late for work.'

'I'm not going,' she said. And Asmir remembered the bombed chocolate factory. His mother was pulling two of everything on to Eldar. He looked like a stuffed bear. But they couldn't put on two pairs of shoes, so Asmir pushed their slippers into his rucksack with the toys.

The telephone rang. 'I'll get it,' Asmir called and ran. He expected to hear Muris's voice. But it was Aunt Melita, ringing from Belgrade. 'I must speak with your mother,' she said and her voice sounded as tight as a guitar string.

Asmir stood close to his mother. He could hear Aunt Melita's words bursting into the familiar room like bullets. 'My newspaper, *Oslobodjenje*, is trying to evacuate women and children on a military plane today. I've put your name on the list. There are already over two hundred people on that list. The plane can only take forty. If you want to be on it you'll have to be at the pick-up point in the city in thirty minutes.'

'But that's three kilometres away!' Mirsada sobbed. 'And Muris has gone to work. Our car's been bombed. There's no public transport and no taxis. And Eldar's sick.'

'It might be your last chance, Mirsada,' Melita urged. 'You've got to try, for the children's sake, and Mother's.'

Then the phone went dead.

Asmir looked at his mother. Her face was strained like a mask, tight and white. 'Tell Grandmother to get ready. We must leave in five minutes.'

Asmir ran to her room. But he didn't have to say anything. She was stuffing clothes into a bag. 'Now?' she asked. He nodded. And ran to the kitchen. Breakfast. He hadn't had breakfast. He gulped down a mug of water and stuffed two rolls into his pockets.

His mother was on the phone again. He leaned against her. He could hear his father saying, 'You can do it, Dada.' He loved the way his father called her Dada. 'You can do it. You must do it. For my sake.'

Then there was cracking and a crash. And the phone went dead again. Asmir hoped with all his heart that it was only the phone which was dead.

His mother was bundling up Eldar into a rug. She put him in Grandmother's arms and picked up the two suitcases. Asmir swung his rucksack on to his back and grabbed Grandmother's bag. The door banged behind them. Their footsteps clattered on the stairs. Asmir pushed open the front door. They hurried out into the scarred and rubble-strewn street.

'We've less than twenty-five minutes to get there,' Mirsada panted, 'before the bus leaves for the airport.'

'Follow me,' Grandmother said. 'There aren't any short cuts in Sarajevo that I don't know. And the alleys will be safer than the main roads.'

She took the lead, threading the way through lanes and courtyards and side streets, turning aside to avoid craters and debris, burned out cars and dead bodies. There wasn't time even to try and recognise friends. She shifted Eldar from hip to hip, and Asmir shifted her bag from hand to hand. His breath was coming in little panting panicky sobs. He felt sick and he wished he hadn't had the water which was sloshing round inside him, very close to the top.

His mother was flagging. Asmir grabbed a case from her with his free hand. The case had little wheels on it but they were no use, no use at all on the rough and broken roadway. Desperately he yanked and tugged. Desperately he wished he was taller, bigger, stronger, older. Daddy! How can I do your job, Daddy? I'm only seven and I feel sick.

The water came up in a sudden gout, splattering over the dark cobbles. Asmir did not even wipe his mouth. He didn't have a free hand now and it would have meant stopping. He was behind already. Behind, behind, behind. Further, further, further. Hurry, hurry, hurry. Faster, faster, faster. Oh Muris, why aren't you here?

His mother was waiting for him to catch up. 'Thank you for giving me a rest. I'll be able to manage now.'

'Are you sure, Dada?' he said.

She smiled at him over her shoulder, already hurrying on again with the two cases. Asmir stumbled on after her, feeling as if his arms were coming out of their sockets.

'We're more than halfway,' Grandmother called back to him. Asmir put on another spurt, though the horse and cart were digging in between his shoulder blades and he was sweating like a real horse under his extra layer and anorak.

He changed hands again, noticing numbly that the bag straps had rubbed his fingers raw.

On and on. Coming to corners. Doubling back painfully when the way was blocked. Hearing the sound of mortars. Seeing the flash of gunfire. Hearing the crash of falling brickwork. Seeing blood and more blood on the road.

Asmir wondered when he would wake up in his own bed. Would the nightmare end soon? If only Muris would reach out and put his arms around him again. Then he heard Muris saying, 'War never does make sense.' And he knew he would not wake up in his own bed again. Ever.

And the tears made it even harder to go on, harder to see the holes, the humps, the hazards. He fell, struggled up, fell again. His breath was coming in choking gasps. He could hear Eldar crying. And Eldar almost never cried. Never.

'Nearly there,' his mother called back. 'One more spurt.'

Asmir didn't think he had another spurt left in him. Not even half a spurt. Then he saw Muris. Muris running towards him. Muris scooping him up, bag and all. Muris running with him in his arms across the finishing line. 'We won,' Asmir said.

'Not yet,' his father said.

Lots of mothers were waiting with their children and piles of bags and bundles. Then a big bus came and everyone started to shove to get aboard. Asmir was glad their father was there. He helped other mothers and grandmothers too, squeezing their things in where it looked as if even a matchbox wouldn't fit.

The bus was almost ready to leave when suddenly soldiers appeared. They grabbed the men who had been helping. They grabbed Asmir's father by the arms. The driver revved the engine and the bus roared off.

Asmir gripped his mother's hand. 'Daddy!' he screamed.

So did thirty other children, and some began to cry. Even Eldar, always cheerful, always smiling until yesterday, began to bawl. There was no room to play peek-a-boo, so Asmir tickled him. Eldar loved being tickled. Even through a jacket, a jumper, a skivvy and a T-shirt he gave a little giggle. His mother smiled at Asmir over his head. 'Thank you, my brave son,' she whispered.

The bus rattled on. Crying subsided into sobbing. Sobbing became hiccups. The children fell asleep in the stuffy jolting capsule. Eldar snuggled up on his mother's lap. Asmir was sitting on Grandmother's knees and they were thin and bony. But she smelled good and he fell asleep too. He woke later to feel his hair damp and Grandmother's tears trickling slowly down his cheeks.

He patted her hands – the hands that made the best stuffed apples in the world – and wondered if the soldiers had let Muris go. He was glad he had put in two photos – one of Muris helping him to blow out the candles on his seventh birthday, and one of Muris holding Eldar on his first. Muris so handsome with his wavy hair and his eyes that laughed.

And every moment the bus took them further and further away from their father.

# 3  Refugees

When the bus stopped at last it was outside a big hangar at the airport. There was gunfire from behind and more gunfire from beyond the fence. Asmir looked for their plane. There were several standing on the tarmac. He wondered which one it would be.

He thought they would all get off the bus and hurry inside the hangar to wait. But the driver refused to open the door. He was talking on his little handset. 'The plane's not here yet. So you have to stay aboard until it arrives,' he told his passengers.

Asmir felt the ripple of fear that ran through all the women. And he felt the fidget of impatience growing into a fever in the frustrated and bored children. Everyone was wedged into the seats like biscuits in a tin. The aisle was piled with bags and boxes. The overhead racks were heavy with rugs and roped-up bundles. There

16

was not a sliver of space to stretch or walk. It was scarcely possible even to wriggle. And the driver would not let them open the windows more than the narrowest crack. So the air became stale and smelly.

Women began to weep as the time dragged on and no plane appeared. Children grew more and more restless and began to cry. 'Please let the children out to relieve themselves,' Asmir's mother asked the driver. 'Just beside the bus,' she pleaded.

At first he refused. But she begged and begged, until at last he gave in. Asmir stood on the step and peed, breathing the outside air that smelled of smoke and burning oil.

Family by family the mothers clambered over the luggage in the aisle to take their children to the door. It was especially hard for the ladies with big baby bellies. Asmir was glad that his mother wasn't like that any more. It was hard enough for her with Eldar in her arms, whining and fretful. She fanned him with her hanky and Asmir played with him to try to stop him crying.

Hour after hour they sat. Pins and needles in the feet gave way to cramp in the legs. Numbness in the bottom became numbness in the heart, and hope turned into sharp icicles of fear. Even the ears became dulled to the sound of mortar bombs, distant and not so far away. And the eyes grew weary with straining for a glimpse of the plane that was supposed to save them.

Asmir produced his two rolls and Mirsada shared them round. But they were tough now and dry, hard to swallow without a drink. Asmir was past being hungry but he gnawed on his crust for something to do. A thick sock of heavy grey cloud had hidden the sun and the afternoon was shrinking steadily. Then suddenly above the sounds of fighting Asmir heard a sound that could have been a plane.

He listened hard and rubbed the fogged-up window with his fist, longing to see the silhouette of their plane on the horizon. He eased the window open another crack. The sound grew louder. It couldn't be mistaken now. It was a plane. A green and grey and brown plane coming in to land.

He nudged Grandmother. She smiled at him. But suddenly Asmir couldn't smile back. This was the plane that was taking them away from Muris.

In a moment they were hurried from the bus and herded into the hangar. It was like a giant's cave, high and hollow and so cold that Asmir's teeth began to chatter. They huddled together for so long that Asmir thought they had been forgotten. Then suddenly they were pushed outside again on to the tarmac in a jostling mob towards the plane.

There was a man in uniform standing at the foot of the gangway leading up to the dark doorway into the plane. 'We'll only take forty,' he said. 'We can't take all of you. Too many kids altogether.'

A moan and a wail went up from the tense tired mothers. Asmir had never heard a sound quite like it. And he never wanted to hear it again. Children began to scream.

Mirsada stepped forward. She spoke in her calm quiet way which made people pause and listen.

'Of course you have regulations. And normally they must be observed. But this is not normal. And you would not be overloading to take more than forty passengers. After all most of them are children, even babies. And it's not as if we have heaps of excess luggage. We've only got what we could carry. There wouldn't be more than one case each. And the children have only got their little carry bags of treasures. Please take us all,' she pleaded. 'Please.'

The man in uniform looked at her and Asmir was proud of her. She was so beautiful with her long dark hair and her big dark eyes. He looked at Eldar in her arms, and Grandmother who had moved up beside her daughter. Grandmother so

19

frail that she wouldn't have weighed as much as some of the bigger children. It was hard to believe how Grandmother had carried Eldar in her arms, leading all the way on that desperate run for their lives only this morning. So frail but so determined.

Then the man looked at Asmir with his jeans torn at the knees, his scuffed dirty shoes; Asmir trying hard not to cry. And suddenly he seemed to see that their hearts were as raw and blistered as their hands.

'All right,' he said gruffly. 'All aboard. And hurry up. We don't want to hang around here. It's not healthy.'

His mother's smile made Asmir think of the lamp with the pink silk shade at home and how it glowed when it was switched on. 'Thank you,' she said to the man, and Asmir and Grandmother said it too. Eldar gave a proper smile for the first time that day.

'God go with you,' the man muttered. Asmir shook his hand, as he had seen Muris do.

Other families were already scrambling aboard, passing up babies and bundles. By the time Asmir and Mirsada and Grandmother got inside with Eldar and their luggage, all the seats were taken and they had to sit on the floor.

Asmir had never been in a plane before. He looked around. It was dim and crowded.

Through a small window he could see the glow of burning buildings in the distance and the flare of tracer bullets in the dark which had come down like a cloak.

The engines started up and the plane vibrated and throbbed. Children screamed again. Mother soothed Eldar and Grandmother patted Asmir's hand. He knew she was smiling at him in the dark. It was strange how you could be so glad and so sad at the same time. And so scared. If only Muris were with them. Muris had flown many times. If only Muris could be here for Asmir's first flight.

Shuddering into action, the plane lumbered along the runway. There was a thump and Asmir knew they were airborne at last. Climbing, climbing. The fires of Sarajevo disappearing into the distance in the south west. Sarajevo. Home. Muris. Oh Muris! Asmir clenched his raw and aching hands. Come soon, Muris! Asmir had never felt so cold before in all his life. Cold cold cold.

## 4 Belgrade

An hour later in Serbia, Aunt Melita and her husband Miroslav were waiting for them at the Belgrade airport. They were journalists. They had come from Sarajevo long before the war started and they had a nice apartment in the city. But already there were eight other people from Sarajevo staying with them. And now with Asmir and Eldar and their mother and grandmother there were fourteen people in the two rooms.

Asmir and Eldar were lucky. They had a little corner all to themselves underneath the palms in pots behind the sofa. It was their own private little jungle. Asmir took out the teddies and arranged the farm animals, pretending the teddies were monkeys, the cows were tigers and the sheep were lions.

Sometimes the corner was smelly in the morning with Eldar. Sometimes Asmir himself needed to go in a hurry and had to creep out past Grandmother on the sofa and over all the people sleeping on the floor. Often he had to wait while other people used the toilet and he would be hopping up and down.

But the houses in Belgrade all had roofs and the windows all had glass. Planes flew across the city and no bombs fell. And the shops still had things to sell, though each day Asmir and his mother had to walk to many before they had enough food to fill their bags. And each week it became more difficult to find, even at the market. War was having its effect in Serbia too, making it hard to get farm products in the towns.

Then one day someone serving Mirsada said, 'You're refugees, aren't you?'

Mirsada stood her ground. 'No,' she said firmly. 'Not at all. We're just visiting my sister and her husband.' She waited for the sausage she had ordered to be cut and wrapped. But Asmir noticed that her fingers were trembling as she picked the coins out of her purse. And he noticed that they did not go back to that shop again.

They walked farther and farther each day.

When they took Eldar to the hospital for his cough, people in the big waiting room gave them unfriendly looks. And when the nurse called

Eldar's name, the man beside them scowled and muttered. Asmir moved closer to his mother. She was holding her head high, but Asmir knew she was upset by the way she gripped his hand. And although the doctor who looked at Eldar was kind, Asmir hoped they wouldn't have to go back there again.

Grandmother was nervous about going out and stayed home with Eldar, keeping the two overcrowded rooms as clean and tidy as possible. She did Melita's washing and took pride in ironing Miroslav's shirts. She read the papers which they brought home, looking for any news of the areas where relatives and friends lived.

Asmir wanted to play in the park at the end of the next street and to take Eldar there. He felt sorry for him, cooped up all day in the little flat, where there wasn't even a balcony.

Mirsada looked serious when he asked. 'I'll come with you,' she said. 'You can't go by yourselves. And when I call, I'll use nicknames.'

'Why must we have different names?' Asmir was puzzled.

'Because your names are Muslim,' his mother said.

Asmir felt scared. And angry too. The war had driven them from their home. It had separated them from their father. Now it was taking his name. And Eldar's.

'What are you going to call us?' he wanted to know. 'I like my name as it is.'

'I thought of Atzo. It's short for Alexander. He was a great king.'

'Atzo.' Asmir repeated it slowly. He liked the thought of borrowing the name of a king. 'What about Eldar?' he asked.

'Edi,' his mother said. 'Short for Edward.'

'Edi in the park,' Asmir said to Eldar. 'Edi on the swings.' And Eldar grinned. He didn't know enough to be scared because he had to have another name if he went outside.

But Asmir was scared. And lonely too. He was missing his friends. He'd seen some boys on the stairs in the apartment block. But they were older. And they obviously didn't want to play with him.

So now he filled his pad with pictures for Muris. And he cut words and letters out of the newspapers after Grandmother and Mirsada had finished reading them, and pasted them in a big scrapbook Aunt Melita had given him.

At night everyone crowded around the TV watching the war in Sarajevo. They saw whole streets of houses burning. Asmir felt his stomach churning every night and every night he wondered if their home was safe. They watched the people as they looked at their bombed houses, carried away the wounded and buried the dead.

Asmir always hoped they would see his father helping someone. But they never did.

Then one night there were pictures of camps full of men taken by the soldiers. Asmir looked fearfully for Muris. But he was not there. He crept in beside his mother later and left Eldar by himself in the corner. It was all right for Eldar because he was always asleep by the time the TV came on. Though he often asked, 'Where's Daddy?' and hugged Uncle Miroslav round the knees. And their mother's eyes looked like dry black lakes.

Two days after the pictures of the camp Aunt Melita had a phone call at her office from a friend in Sarajevo, who rang to tell them that he had seen Muris in the street that very morning. The soldiers had cut most of the telephone lines and it was lucky he could get through. But he promised to ring again when he next saw their father.

Mirsada smiled and hugged Asmir. Asmir felt so happy. And when Eldar said again, 'Where's Daddy?' he showed him the photos and said, 'Here's Daddy!'

But that night on TV there were pictures of people in buses and trains and cars. And talk of refugees. Escaping the war in Sarajevo. Refugees. Asmir asked his mother, 'Are we refugees too?'

Mirsada said, 'Not really.' Then she added

27

what she had said to the shop assistant. 'We came to see Aunt Melita and Uncle Miroslav.'

Each night there were more pictures of soldiers and bombed houses, old men hobbling to buses, old women crying in trains, and sad-faced mothers with children. And more talk of refugees. But never a picture of Muris.

Then one night the screen showed pictures of men in uniform, who looked like soldiers, standing in front of big gates across a road. The man on TV said that the border crossings might soon be closed. And everyone fell very silent.

Asmir wanted to ask what border crossings were, but his aunt and uncle had begun talking in low voices to Mother and Grandmother.

'I think it's time,' Aunt Melita was saying.

Time for what? Asmir wondered.

Grandmother was patting Mother. 'It's weeks since there's been milk for Eldar here. And months since Asmir has had any. There's nothing you can do for Muris except look after the children. You must think of them first.'

Mirsada nodded dumbly and her eyes were oceans glittering with tears.

Uncle Miroslav was saying, 'I'll try to get petrol tomorrow on the black market, and if there's any to be had we'll leave on Sunday.'

Asmir tugged Melita. 'Are we real refugees now?'

'Not yet,' his aunt said. 'Besides, we're lucky. We've got a friend to go to. In Vienna. His name is Chris. He's public affairs manager for a big car manufacturer. I've done a lot of work for him over the last two years.'

'Why do we have to go?' Asmir asked.

Aunt Melita explained. 'Once they close the borders, we won't be able to leave Serbia. And it's not safe here any more for any of us.'

'Not safe in Belgrade?' Asmir asked. There were no bombs here, no soldiers. 'Why isn't it safe?' Asmir remembered the suspicious questions, the ugly stares, his new name.

'Because we're Muslims,' Aunt Melita said. Aunt Melita sounded sad and angry and hurt all at the same time, and he understood. He hugged her. She was so pretty in her silky flowery dress, with her long curly brown-gold hair and her big grey-blue eyes. He hated to see the glint of tears behind the shining frames of her glasses. She was always so bright and cheerful about everything.

'But Uncle Miroslav isn't,' he said. 'He's Serbian so that ought to be all right.' Uncle Miroslav was as solid as a rock, quiet and sure of himself and of what to do. He had to be. Otherwise he wouldn't have been in charge of one of the biggest sections in the main news service in Belgrade.

'No, and that makes it worse, not better, because other Serbs won't trust him.'

Asmir was puzzled. No wonder his father had said, 'War never does make sense.'

'Is Vienna far away?' he asked.

Aunt Melita nodded. 'We'll have to drive all day and half the night. We have four borders to cross, out of Serbia, into Hungary, out of Hungary and into Austria.'

It sounded a difficult journey to Asmir. 'How will Father find us?'

'He will,' Aunt Melita said.

And Asmir believed her.

## 5  Crossing the Borders

Next day Asmir helped pack again. It didn't take long. There wasn't much. It didn't take Aunt Melita and Uncle Miroslav long either, because there wasn't much room in the car. It was only a little car, just right for two people, but a real squash for six, even without luggage and the extra can of petrol Uncle Miroslav had managed to get.

So Aunt Melita and Uncle Miroslav left everything in their lovely apartment – the paintings on the walls, the books on the shelves, the china in the cupboards, the quilts on the bed, the clothes in the wardrobe. There was only room in the car for a case of clothes each and some food and drink for the journey.

Sunday was hot. Much too hot for Asmir and Eldar or anyone to wear two layers of clothes. Asmir's mother didn't want to leave anything behind. What they had brought from Sarajevo was all they had. So Miroslav packed and re-packed the car and managed to squeeze in everything and everybody. Even Muris couldn't have done better if he had been there, Asmir told his uncle. And Aunt Melita joked that it was just as well she had got so thin in the last few months.

But nobody joked about how thin Grand-mother had become. Nobody said anything about that. She was as thin and as brittle as a wafer biscuit. Sitting on her lap, Asmir was afraid she might snap under his weight. But she was still all sweet inside, and she hugged Asmir and helped him forget for a moment as they set off that they were refugees.

They hadn't gone more than twenty kilo-metres when the car broke down.

'Surely not the radiator boiling with such a load?' Aunt Melita said.

'Dirty petrol more likely,' Uncle Miroslav muttered. 'You never know what rubbish they put in this black market stuff. Everybody had better get out. I'll have to drain the line and I don't know how long it will take.'

There was no shade, but the sunflowers in the field beside the road were like a forest to Asmir. He wanted to crawl in and make a cubby for Eldar and Grandmother among the tall green stems. But his mother said it wouldn't be fair to the farmer. So they stretched a rug between the opened doors and made a little shelter.

Asmir passed tools to his uncle as he knelt beside the engine, adjusting and unscrewing nuts. He looked at the sunflowers. A few bees moved slowly over their big rough centres that were like rounds of black bread, while a furry bumble bee droned in the clover. The butterflies rested with folded wings, looking like brown leaves. A ladybird suddenly opened its shiny shell, spread its wings and took off.

Mirsada passed round a bottle of water. 'Just one swallow each. It's got to last.'

How long? Asmir wondered. But did not ask.

Uncle Miroslav spat out the last mouthful of dirty petrol from the fuel hose and wiped his beard. Mother gave him a cup of water and half an apple. The other half she divided carefully among the five of them.

Uncle Miroslav switched on the ignition. The car started and they all scrambled in. It was as hot as a pizza pan and smelled horribly of petrol. Crouched on Grandmother's knees, Asmir felt sweaty and sick. 'When are we going to get there?' he asked.

'Not for a long time yet. We won't even reach the first border for a couple of hours. We hope they'll let us through into Hungary. We'll say we're going on holidays,' Aunt Melita said.

'Just as well I've got my holiday rucksack,' Asmir said. 'And just as well you put it on top,' he said to his uncle.

Uncle Miroslav grinned at him in the rear vision mirror. But nobody said anything. Asmir knew they were praying. Except for Eldar of course, who was asleep. But the soldiers had bombed God. How could He hear their prayers? Asmir felt very lonely. And Muris? He wanted his father. And his father's mother, his other grandmother? Was she all right? Could she and Muris look after each other?

Hungary. A foreign country. What if they don't let us through? Asmir wondered. Do we go back and unpack again? He looked in the mirror and Uncle Miroslav's face was grim now. Aunt Melita's eyes were closed and so were Grandmother's. And tears were running slowly out of Mother's into Eldar's curls.

So what if they don't? Asmir asked himself again. What if the border crossing is closed? And he thought of his train set that he had left at home and the barriers that came down across the road if a train was crossing.

Eldar woke and began to chatter. But even Aunt Melita, who was always cheerful and smiling, did not take any notice, and after a while he also fell silent. Asmir knew that his little brother too could feel the fear for all that was unknown ahead.

The car was so slow with its heavy load. Other cars full of people passed, and trucks and buses too. 'I hope there's not a long queue at the border,' Aunt Melita said, voicing one of the fears they all had.

But when at last Uncle Miroslav slowed right down at the first signs, there were only two trucks and a bus ahead, and they went into a different specially marked lane. The guard waved the car on.

'We're through!' Asmir shouted.

'Not yet,' Aunt Melita said. 'We're only out of Serbia. We still have to get into Hungary. But we don't know if they'll let us in.'

She had hardly said it before there were buildings with a different flag, more signs in letters that were different from those Asmir knew, words in another language. More barricades, more men in different uniforms who looked uncomfortably like soldiers.

One of them signalled Uncle Miroslav to stop. He looked into the car and scowled. He did not even smile at Eldar. Asmir felt sorry for any little boys at his house. He didn't look as if he would be the sort of father Asmir knew. He wasn't kind and friendly like Muris. He growled something Asmir could not understand and Uncle Miroslav handed over all the precious passports.

The man turned on his heel without another word and disappeared into one of the buildings where there were other men in uniform.

They sat and waited. And waited. And waited.

They waited so long that Asmir wanted to pee. He whispered to his mother. She shook her head. 'Not yet,' Mirsada whispered back, as if any word or movement might make the bad-tempered man come stomping out of the grey building and point them back the way they had come.

Asmir squeezed his legs together tightly. The border guard came out at last, frowning, the precious passports clenched in his right hand. He

shoved them at Uncle Miroslav, waving the car on with his left.

Uncle Miroslav switched on the ignition. Everyone let out a sigh. Asmir let out something else as well. Suddenly Grandmother's lap felt damp. He looked at her and his cheeks went hot. 'Sorry, Grandma,' he whispered. She smiled and hugged him hard. He knew he had the best grandmother in the world.

## 6 Further and Further

No one spoke while they drove on into Hungary.
As the kilometres stretched out behind them
Asmir knew they were going further and further
away from his father. From Muris.

Further and further. They passed fields and
fields of sunflowers and villages of yellow-painted
houses. Asmir saw a farmer with his horse and
cart and was glad he'd put in the toy one which
Muris had given Eldar for his first birthday.

Mirsada handed out pieces of bread. But they
were hard and dry, and Asmir couldn't swallow.
They passed cherry trees bright with fruit and
busy with people balancing baskets on ladders.
They saw people selling cherries by the roadside.

But Uncle Miroslav wouldn't stop. He didn't
want to stop before they had reached the border
and were safely through into Austria. Besides,
they didn't have the right sort of money.

Asmir longed for the juicy sweetness of the

cherries and thought of the trees at home in Sarajevo. He hoped his father was getting some cherries.

On and on they drove. Asmir said, 'When are we going to get there?'

'Later,' Aunt Melita said. 'After it is dark.'

'Where are we going when we get there?'

'Our friend Chris has offered us his apartment while he takes his parents for a holiday for three weeks. They are visiting from Australia.'

'What will we do when they come back?'

'Then Chris's friend Matthias has offered us his apartment for a month. It's all arranged,' Aunt Melita reassured him.

Asmir wondered where they would go after Matthias came home, but that wouldn't be for a little while. So he asked about a much closer worry. 'If it's dark when we get there, how will we find Chris's apartment?'

'Matthias is coming in his car to meet us on the *Autobahn*, the highway, before we reach Vienna, to show us the way.'

'Even though it will be the middle of the night?'

'Yes,' said Aunt Melita. 'Aren't we lucky to have such good friends!'

'Do Chris and Matthias speak Serbo-Croatian like us?'

'No. Chris is Australian. He speaks English

and German. Matthias is Austrian. He speaks German and English,' Aunt Melita explained.

'How will I say "Thank you" to them?'

'I can teach you the English,' Aunt Melita said. 'But I don't know any German either. So we'll all have to learn that together, because the people in Austria all speak German.'

Asmir was beginning to feel very confused. But he repeated 'Thank you,' in English after her. Then, 'My name is Asmir. I am seven years old. My brother is Eldar. He is sixteen months old.'

His mother said, 'My name is Mirsada. We come from Sarajevo. The children's father is still there.'

Asmir was surprised to hear his mother speaking English. His aunt said, 'Your mother knows English, but she is shy speaking it because she has not used it for so long. We shall all have to practise.'

On and on they drove, kilometre after kilometre, through fields of maize and wheat stretching across the plain as far as they could see in the bright sunlight.

'When are we going to get there?' Asmir asked again.

'After the sun goes down and the moon comes up,' Aunt Melita said.

Half afraid, half glad, Asmir watched the fiery

sunset. Then just as the moon was rising like a shining golden coin, he saw some deer in a wheatfield. They looked so beautiful against the sky. He was happy there were no men hiding with guns to shoot them.

The moon rose higher and higher. Asmir wondered if his father was watching it too. It grew smaller and smaller, further and further away. He looked at his mother. Her face was so sad. He knew she was thinking of Muris too. He lifted a strand of sweaty hair from her cheek and smiled at her. 'Muris will be all right, Dada,' he said stoutly for both of them. And she smiled at him.

Then a cloud came across the sky and hid it. Asmir shivered and Grandmother hugged him.

'Are we nearly there?'

'Not yet,' Aunt Melita said.

Asmir yawned. Eldar was already asleep. But he was only a baby. Asmir said, 'My name is Asmir. I am seven years old. My brother's name is Eldar. He is sixteen months old.'

'Very good,' Aunt Melita said.

'Thank you,' said Asmir.

Grandmother stroked his hair and he fell asleep. He woke suddenly as the car was slowing down. 'Are we there?'

'Not yet,' Aunt Melita replied. And Asmir

knew before she said it. 'This is the border into Austria.'

He could feel the fear from all the grown-ups pressing in. It was so heavy he could hardly breathe.

On the Hungarian side the border guard waved them through.

'Glad to get rid of us,' Uncle Miroslav muttered.

There was a red and white flag ahead. Red was Muris's favourite colour. There were more signs in strange letters, more buildings, yet more men in uniform. One stepped out in front of the car.

Asmir could feel Grandmother holding her breath. As the guard came to Uncle Miroslav's window everyone was holding their breath. Everyone except Eldar. He was still asleep.

Would they be allowed to pass?

Or would they be turned back? To Serbia?

The guard looked into the car. He saw Eldar and smiled. He saw Asmir and smiled again. He saw Grandmother and bowed. He handed back the passports Uncle Miroslav had given him and waved them on.

Miroslav drove across the border. The border into Austria – *Oesterreich*. Where there was no war . . . And no Muris. Where there was milk for Eldar. And for Asmir too. And meat and eggs and bread and butter and cheese. Perhaps God might still be here too.

Everybody was laughing and crying. Even Aunt Melita was crying. Asmir kissed Grandmother. He leaned over and kissed Aunt Melita too. He kissed his mother and tasted the salt of the tears on her cheeks. She was smiling but he knew she was thinking about Muris. Muris alone so far away in Sarajevo.

Uncle Miroslav had not stopped driving. But his shoulders were not hunched any more and his knuckles were not showing white through his skin. Asmir planted a kiss on his bald patch. 'Thank you, Uncle Miroslav.'

# 7  *Safe At Last*

The moon came out from behind the cloud and Asmir fell asleep. He woke again when the car slowed down and pulled off the wide *Autobahn*. There were lights, the sound of voices and people laughing, the smell of petrol and coffee. Uncle Miroslav got out of the car. And a tall man stepped out of a big car parked by the roadhouse. He walked across to Miroslav smiling and holding out his hand.

'Welcome to Austria! I am Matthias.'

He came to the car and bowed to Grandmother and Mother and kissed Aunt Melita's cheek. He smiled at Asmir, who said in English, 'My name is Asmir. I am seven years old. Thank you, Matthias.'

Matthias pointed to his car and said in English, 'Would you like to come with me?'

Asmir looked at his aunt. Melita said, 'Matthias is inviting you to go in his car while he guides us into Vienna and takes us to Chris's apartment.'

Asmir looked at his mother. Mirsada nodded. He said, 'Thank you,' to Matthias and climbed off Grandmother's lap out of the car. Matthias's car was dark gleaming red. The seat was so big there would have been room for his mother as well. He stretched out his legs and wriggled and wriggled on the soft upholstery.

Matthias smiled. 'Do you want to go to sleep?' Asmir did not understand his language so Matthias cradled his head on his hands.

But Asmir shook his head. It was much too exciting. There was so much to see even though it was night, with the cars rushing by. The lights were as bright as day along the *Autobahn* and in the distance they shone and winked from tall buildings. And there was lovely music coming from the car radio. Happy music that made Asmir want to dance. He wished his mother could hear it. Matthias passed him a chocolate bar and Asmir felt happier than he had been for a long long time.

They entered a big city where the wide tree-lined streets were without bomb craters, buildings stood in tall undamaged rows and lights glowed comfortingly. Every so often Asmir looked behind to be sure that Uncle Miroslav was still following.

They turned off the broad streets into a narrow one, made even narrower by cars parked on each side. Asmir could see the lights of Uncle Miroslav's car. Round a corner. Then another. And another.

How would his father Muris ever find this place when he escaped from Bosnia?

Matthias was slowing down. There was an empty space in front of a high archway with a solid wooden door. He waved Uncle Miroslav into it. 'Here we are,' he said.

Asmir knew, even though Matthias said it in English, that they had arrived at last. He was glad. But sorry too to leave the big smooth car and the dancing music. 'Thank you,' he said.

Uncle Miroslav was standing on the pavement, stretching. Aunt Melita was taking Eldar, still asleep, from Mirsada. Matthias was helping Grandmother out of the car. Everyone was stretching after the long cramped anxious journey.

Matthias unlocked the big door and as they unpacked the car they began carrying the luggage through a lofty arcade into a cobbled courtyard. Matthias opened a door into a hallway, then opened another door.

It was a lift. They stacked the cases and bundles into it with Grandmother, Mother and Eldar. Matthias pointed to the stairs and held up two fingers. Asmir ran ahead up two flights and arrived just as the lift did. He helped Grandmother out and then started pulling out the luggage.

Matthias arrived with the keys to Chris's apartment. He opened another door and pressed the switch. Lights sprang alive, twinkling their welcome, banishing the long darkness. Asmir kicked off his shoes, ran down the passage barefoot over the shining floor, round the corner into another passage and on into a big big room where the lights hung in great bouquets of glittering crystal from the high high ceiling.

He smiled at everyone as they followed him into the room. Eldar was awake now, laughing and calling out. He scrambled out of his mother's arms and began running with Asmir from room to room. Round and round they ran, dizzy with delight. They hardly even stopped for the milk which their mother had found in the refrigerator. They rocked in the rocking chair and clinked on the grand piano.

Then they found the bathroom, gleaming white with cool marble walls and floor. Asmir turned on the gold taps over the big big bath and they peeled off their clothes, climbing in, laughing and splashing. They didn't want to get out when Mother came with towels. But Mirsada told them there was a bag of toys that Chris's

parents had left specially for them. So they hopped out and put on their pyjamas.

There was a panda and a puppy, which they put to bed straightaway on the couch their mother had pulled out and made up with sheets and blankets. There was a soft ball with a bell inside which tinkled as they tossed it. And there were coloured quoits which they stacked and restacked. Eldar put them on the peg in any order, but Asmir made sure each time they went from the biggest on the bottom to the smallest on the top.

They were having so much fun they didn't want to go to bed. But when Mirsada lay down on the couch in her nightdress and pulled up the blanket, Asmir turned off the big chandeliers and they both snuggled in beside their mother. Then Asmir wished with all his heart that Muris was on his other side.

He woke to the sound of bells greeting the new day. He crept out of bed and tiptoed to the window, leaning out to listen and look. The sound of the biggest bell rolled over him and through him. It was sweet and warm and thick like the dark chocolate icing on his birthday cake. Other bells were chiming and tinkling, silvery like the little balls his mother used for his name. Still others danced and flickered like the seven red candles.

The soldiers hadn't bombed God here. Asmir wanted to shout and sing with the bells. He wanted to dance across the shining sunlit floor. He wanted to rock in the chair and crash on the piano.

But everyone else was still asleep. So he hugged his secret joy silently and stared around the big room which would be home for three weeks.

He examined the pattern of the parquetry floor, hundreds and hundreds of blocks of wood set in smooth lines and designs, like tiles in a mosque. He looked at the plants, the palms, the ivy and the ribbon grass. He looked at the pictures of mountains and lakes, of flowers and trees, and two swans wearing crowns, and a lady with dark eyes like his mother's, who seemed to be watching him wherever he went.

He tiptoed into the room where Grandmother was asleep on a mattress on the floor and where there were shelves of books and photos of kangaroos and koalas and a calendar with dolphins on it. Then he crept into the big bedroom where Aunt Melita and Uncle Miroslav were sleeping and looked at the pictures there of boats and people, and out at the pink geraniums on the window ledge above the courtyard.

He looked around the bathroom. 'My name

is Asmir,' he said in English to the seven boys in the mirrors. Asmir. Asmir. Asmir. Asmir. Asmir. Asmir. Asmir. Seven boys smiled back at him.

He pranced along the passage to the door where coats were hanging, house slippers were ranged in a tidy row and big black umbrellas stood in a corner. Then into the toilet. Not having to wait for anyone. Not having to hurry for people waiting to come after him. He washed his hands in the basin, looking at himself in the big red-framed mirror.

On the shelf above there was a pretty goblet full of raspberry jelly and cream with a cherry on top. It seemed a funny place to leave it. He reached up and touched it with his finger for just a little lick.

Then he began to laugh. It was a trick candle. He laughed so much he had to sit on the toilet. Then he crept to the kitchen to fetch a spoon to put beside it.

He had a drink of milk and found some crunchy brown biscuits. Then he crept back into bed beside his mother. Mirsada put her hand out and stroked his hair. And he fell asleep.

## 8  Exploring

The bells of Vienna were ringing again when he woke. Eldar was chattering and his mother was stretching. Uncle Miroslav was whistling in the shower, Aunt Melita and Grandmother were talking in the kitchen and the smell of coffee was floating out.

They sat around the kitchen table eating bread and butter and cheese and sausage and eggs. And there were four different sorts of jam in plastic buckets. They talked and laughed and ate again and drank coffee and milk with chocolate in it. It was like a party. Except that Muris was not there. Asmir saw Mirsada looking at the empty chair beside the wall and knew what she was wishing.

It was already afternoon when they went downstairs across the cobbled courtyard out through the big gateway into the narrow street with its long name – *Sonnenfelsgasse*.

There was a shop window with some smart furniture and a long row of teddy bears which had all been much loved – big ones, little ones, medium ones, shabby and worn. The biggest one was sitting up in a toy car which could have taken Eldar and they all laughed again.

Asmir thought of the long journey. It was only yesterday that they'd all been squashed in the little car. And now their teddies were sitting up in the big room under the glittering chandeliers with the swans for company and the lady to watch that they didn't get into mischief.

The shop windows were full of all sorts of things to buy and people were walking along eating ice-creams or pizza, or sitting at tables along the pavement, drinking coffee. It looked just as Sarajevo had looked before the soldiers came. Asmir felt at home.

Then he heard his favourite bell again. He tugged his mother's hand and they started to walk towards the sound. The last echoes were just dying away when they came out into a big open square. The tallest building Asmir had ever seen rose up from the middle, towering above all the other buildings, its spire spiking straight up to the summer sky. He caught his breath.

'This is *Stephansplatz*,' Aunt Melita said. She had been to Vienna before. 'And that is *Stephansdom*. The Viennese are very proud of their

cathedral. They have a pet name for it. They call it *Steffl*.'

Asmir looked up at *Steffl*'s great arched doorway and the huge pointed window above it. He had never seen anything like it. As they walked around, he tilted his head right back to look at the roof with its picture of a big black two-headed eagle on the green and yellow tiles.

But Eldar was squealing with delight about something else. With four feet right on the ground. On the roadway was a row of horses, each pair harnessed to its own carriage. Brown horses, black horses, dapple-grey horses. And a special pair Asmir knew at once were his own very favourite.

They were white with big black spots like painted horses on a merry-go-round. They had bright yellow headbands with earpieces to match the yellow trim on the carriage and the spokes on the wheels, which made Asmir think of the sunflowers. And on the carriage door was a double-headed silver eagle.

There were dogs on the pavement too – little low dogs being pulled along like toys by people, and big strong dogs pulling people along like toys. There were poodles with ribbons between their ears and West Highland terriers with tartan collars. There was even an enormous dog licking an ice-cream held out for it by its owner.

But it was the horses Asmir loved. He walked along the line of carriages, looking at them all. Watching people with cameras climbing into them. Watching the drivers in their black bowler hats taking up the reins and the horses obeying their commands. Listening to the sound of the wheels on the cobbles and the laughter from the people as they jolted into motion.

Asmir longed to be sitting up in a carriage – any carriage – smiling and waving to the passers-by and looking out on to the driver's back, watching the horses' rumps swaying. But most of all he longed to be in the carriage with the sunflower wheels and the merry-go-round horses. If Muris were here Asmir was sure that was where they would be. He looked hopefully at Uncle Miroslav.

Miroslav laughed and said, 'It's just as well we had our car for the trip. If we were in one of these, we'd be on the way for weeks.'

Then Asmir remembered. They were refugees. Not tourists. Money was for milk and meat and bread and butter. There was no money for rides in carriages and fancy things. He was glad it didn't cost anything to look.

But Uncle Miroslav said, 'Today we're celebrating! We'll all have ice-cream.' Asmir chose strawberry and savoured every lick to the very last drop. Mirsada chose chocolate and Asmir thought she was probably thinking of the chocolates she used to bring home from the factory in Sarajevo.

On the way back they went into a supermarket. Asmir thought he had never seen so much food before. Aunt Melita bought milk and meat and bread and butter. Uncle Miroslav bought bananas and cherries. The plastic bag cut Asmir's fingers but he was proud to be helping to carry things home.

Next day Aunt Melita went to work in Chris's office. She had worked part-time for him in Belgrade and he had arranged a position for her here in his car firm in Vienna. But Uncle Miroslav had no work to go to. He had to stay home with Grandmother and Mother and the children. And he was restless already, missing his job at the busy news service.

In the afternoon Mirsada took the boys to do the shopping. Eldar wanted to stop and look at the horses. But Asmir held him by the hand and they walked slowly with their mother to the supermarket. Eldar wanted to touch everything and kept picking up things and putting them in the trolley.

'No,' Asmir would say. 'Put it back.'

Eldar laughed and ran off – round a counter piled with cartons of eggs. Asmir grabbed him. But Eldar wriggled free and ran off again between the shelves stacked with jam in jars. Asmir chased him, but Eldar ducked behind the shelves laughing and disappeared. Scared of hearing a crash, Asmir hunted for him. But Eldar bobbed up over the other side near the refrigerated stands of milk and yoghurt. He seized a yoghurt.

'No, Eldar. Put it back,' Asmir called.

But it was too late. Eldar had stuck his finger through the foil. He wailed as Asmir caught up with him and took the yoghurt away. Asmir led him back to their mother, holding out the damaged container. Mirsada looked at it ruefully and put it into the trolley. She looked in her purse at the money Aunt Melita had given her and put back the lettuce she had just chosen.

It was a slow walk home with the shopping bags and Eldar tugging all the time. They stopped again to look at the horses and Asmir was delighted to see his favourite pair waiting patiently by the kerb. He wished he had an apple or a sugar lump to give them. Shyly he smiled at the driver who let him pat their noses. They were warm and hard and Asmir felt the whiffle of their hot breath as he took his hand away.

# 9 The Storm

Next day when they went out Eldar couldn't be dragged beyond the horses. Asmir felt quite embarrassed at his yelling. They walked along the row of horses. Eldar liked a black pair with red headbands and earpieces. He stood happily looking at them while Asmir watched the driver putting up the carriage hood, covering his hat with plastic, and putting a rain cape over his smart waistcoat. The driver was just unfolding big checked coats for the horses when the dark sky lit up with a great flash. There was a rumble and roar like a bomb exploding.

Eldar cried out in fear and Asmir grabbed him, ducking for cover from the heavy stinging raindrops coming as fast as snipers' bullets. Mirsada shepherded them towards *Steffl*'s protecting walls.

People were running for shelter in all directions and in the scramble Asmir and Eldar were separated from their mother. They were swept along into the cathedral porch. Asmir did not realise that Mirsada was not behind them. Then as more and more people crowded in out of the storm they were pushed further and further in. Even though Asmir gripped Eldar as tightly as he could, Eldar was pulled away from him in the surge which went through the doorway.

Asmir was pushed onward too and when he found himself suddenly inside the great building, for the moment he quite forgot Eldar. He forgot his mother. He forgot everything.

He gasped in wonder as he looked up to the ceiling so high above and along the rows of towering pillars, like an avenue of forest giants. A sheet of lightning lit the tall windows at the far end and it was as if all the contents of a queen's jewel box cascaded forth in glittering richness. But most of all it was the stillness and the silence that made Asmir's heart sing.

Over the roll of thunder outside, above all the clatter of feet on the stone floor and the conversation of the rain-drenched tourists inside, there was a peace and a calm that Asmir had never felt before. Even before the soldiers came to Sarajevo. For a moment he stood enfolded in it, wondering at it, wanting to hold it to himself forever.

Then he remembered Eldar. 'Look after Eldar,' Muris had said.

Where was Eldar?

'Eldar,' he called. But panic had closed his throat and no sound came out. Frantically he began to push his way through the crowd. But the legs were as close as stalks in a sunflower field.

'Eldar,' he sobbed. 'Oh, don't let me lose Eldar. Where are you, Eldar?' But the people pressed in on all sides and he couldn't see anything. He wriggled and pushed, not knowing which direction he was going. And suddenly came to a wall.

Oh, where was Eldar? Where had he gone? Please let me find him, he breathed.

Then above the hubbub of the tourists he heard Eldar laugh. He followed the sound, running across the old worn paving. Eldar!

He let out a sigh of relief. Thunder rolled and lightning flashed. And Eldar darted towards something that had caught his notice. There was a stand with myriads of little twinkling candles – one of the prettiest sights Asmir could remember. And obviously Eldar thought so too. He stood there, smiling and chortling.

Asmir saw the picture of a woman above. A woman with a solemn baby. She had dark eyes like his mother and there was sorrow on her face

too. Like those of the mothers with their babies
on the bus from Sarajevo.

Then he saw Eldar reaching out to take
a little white candle from the box below the
stand. Asmir wanted to light the candle and
put it in the stand to twinkle and gleam. He
wanted it more than anything in the world

at that moment. Except Muris, except his father.

But there was a box for money there too. And they had no money. Refugees don't have money for pretty things like candles. 'Put it back, Eldar. We can't have it.'

But Eldar would not put it back. So Asmir took it from him and put it back. Eldar began to wail and Asmir tried to pull him away. A woman nearby took some coins from her purse and dropped them clinking into the box. She picked up a candle and gave it to Asmir. He looked up at her and wished he knew the words to thank her for her kindness. He smiled at her and so did Eldar.

She watched while Asmir lit it carefully from another one and placed it right in the middle of a row. She patted them both on the head and murmured something, then turned away. They watched their candle burning and Asmir thought of Muris.

Then he remembered their mother. Where was she? She would be wondering where they were. He took Eldar's hand as they walked to the big door. Outside the cobbles were gleaming from the rain and people were moving from doorways. Asmir could see their mother coming. Mirsada, bedraggled and worried, was looking for them.

She smiled with relief to see them. 'I worried about you. But you're dry. Where did you get to? What did you do?'

'I'll show you where we went,' Asmir said. He took her shopping bag and led the way in through the great porch, on through the door.

It was just as wonderful the second time as it had been the first. And it had the same effect on his mother as it had on him. She drew in her breath and they stood and gazed. Then Eldar tugged them towards the candles.

Their candle was still burning, low but with a bright steady flame. Asmir told his mother how the kind woman had given it to them. Then she looked up and saw the other sad mother above the candles. Tears began to roll down her cheeks.

Another woman with a kind face came up to them. 'Our father is in Sarajevo,' Asmir said.

'Sarajevo!' the woman said, and a look as sad as the mother's in the picture passed over her face. She patted Eldar and Asmir and put her arms around their mother. And Asmir felt tears burning behind his eyes. Had the soldiers killed his father? Oh, don't let them kill Muris.

That night Aunt Melita came home smiling. She had had another phone call at the office from her contact in Sarajevo. He had seen Muris that day.

# 10 Refugees Again

For the next three days Uncle Miroslav wandered miserably round the apartment. He was used to going to the news service office every day to sit at his desk, ring people for interviews, write articles and prepare the news. But he could not be a journalist in Vienna because he did not have a work permit.

He took Asmir exploring the city. They could walk much farther without Eldar and heavy shopping bags. They found a park where roses of many colours were filling the air with their scent. Asmir liked the red ones best because they were his father's favourite.

They sat on a seat and watched the pigeons strutting and pouting, preening and pecking along the path. And they watched the people with their dogs – old dogs, young dogs, good dogs, naughty dogs, slow dogs, dogs that sniffed at every post, dogs that barked at all the others. Asmir liked watching the naughty dogs best.

They found a playground too with a bench under a big chestnut tree where Uncle Miroslav could sit while Asmir climbed and slid and swung. And the horses and carriages clopped by. Asmir always looked for his horses, but he didn't see them again. And he wondered how he could help Uncle Miroslav find work. But he couldn't think of a way.

He voiced another of his worries to Uncle Miroslav. 'Will it be hard for Muris to find a job too, when he comes?'

Uncle Miroslav looked serious. He paused before he answered. Asmir guessed it was not because he did not know the answer. It was because he did not want to say it. 'Probably, Asmir,' he said after a long moment. 'It's hard when you have a special profession. There's not likely to be much demand for the services of a Bosnian lawyer in Austria. Just as there's no place for a Yugoslav journalist who doesn't speak German. It's one of the problems refugees have to face.'

Then Aunt Melita came home on Friday night with news. Chris and Matthias had arranged a job for Miroslav. It wasn't the sort of work he was used to. Not at all. That just was not possible.

But it was work. And he would be paid. Not

as much as he used to earn as a journalist of course. Uncle Miroslav stroked his silver beard as he considered it. But he was glad to have the chance to do something to earn some money to look after the family he now had.

On Monday he got up at five o'clock to get to the garage to start work by seven. That night he was tired and stiff from stretching and bending and reaching and lifting. And sunburnt too from working outside. It was very different from working in an office. But it was a start.

On Thursday Aunt Melita came home with more news. Milan, another journalist she and Chris knew in Sarajevo, had sent a message. His wife Vesna and son George, who had also got away from Sarajevo and reached Belgrade, were leaving on Friday. They hoped to get through into Austria by train. And he'd asked Aunt Melita to look after them when they arrived in Vienna.

So on Saturday morning Aunt Melita and Uncle Miroslav went to the railway station. The train was packed with refugees – old people, women and children. They found Vesna and George in the crowd and drove them to the apartment. Everyone sat around drinking coffee, talking and listening, eager to hear about the old life and the new.

Vesna said, 'Things have got much worse in

Sarajevo. Our little restaurant was bombed and its stores in the cellar were looted the same day. And of course I had already shut my dress shop because I couldn't get any stock. But one of the worst things is the water shortage. The mains have been bombed and there's no supply to houses any more. Even so, my mother still wouldn't leave. I wish she had come with us.' She pushed back her blond hair and looked at Grandmother, then at Melita and Mirsada. 'You are lucky to be together. If only my mother was here,' she sighed. And Asmir knew how she was feeling.

George said, 'In fact there are only a couple of places in the city where you can still get water. You have to take your buckets and queue for it. Not much fun in this hot weather, I can tell you. I did it for Grandmother as well as for us. I don't know how she'll be managing now. I suppose Dad's doing it for her.'

Asmir looked at George. He was fourteen, tall and solid, almost as big as Uncle Miroslav. Yet even he had found carrying the water difficult. Asmir wondered how his other grandmother was managing. Was Muris fetching water for his mother as well?

Grandmother said, 'It's lovely having someone else to talk to in our own language, even if it's all bad news we hear. Our own language

is one of the things I miss most here. I don't think I'll ever learn German well enough to have a good conversation,' she sighed.

Vesna and George showed their two treasured photos of Milan. They hadn't seen him for months. And they had no news of Muris. Asmir could see his own disappointment mirrored in his mother's face.

Soon Vesna and George were falling asleep at the table, because they had been sitting up all night in the train. So Melita put them to bed in Chris's room and shut the door. And Asmir stopped Eldar from playing on the piano. Then their mother took them out for a walk so that Eldar would go to sleep for a while afterwards too.

Asmir thought about George. Was he missing his father terribly too? Did he also have nightmares? He looked forward to George waking up.

He hoped George would play with him and Eldar. And he did.

On Sunday when Aunt Melita and Uncle Miroslav took the whole family to a big park called the *Prater*, George pushed the swings and swung too. Although he was so grown-up in the way he looked after his mother, he seemed really glad to do childish things again. He went on the see-saw with Asmir and Eldar and followed them up and down the slides. It was like having a big brother.

Then it was their last week in Chris's apartment. Mother and Grandmother and Vesna cleaned and polished everything and everywhere so that there was not a footmark or finger smear to be seen, or a speck of dust. They even washed the leaves of the house plants.

Uncle Miroslav had got so used to polishing cars that he decided he would do something extra and very special. With Aunt Melita's help he cleaned all the windows.

They were big casement windows in pairs, double glazed. Uncle Miroslav climbed out onto the ledge and lifted each one off its hinges. One by one he carried them into the bathroom where Aunt Melita washed them in the shower. Asmir stood by, handing dry towels and helping to rub the glass shining dry. And he thought of Muris and Milan carrying water home in buckets along the dangerous streets of Sarajevo.

And he remembered how he had helped to stick tapes criss-cross over the windows to try to reduce the danger from shattering. Were the windows still whole? Was the house still there?

'When will the war end?' he asked Aunt Melita. 'When can we go home?'

'I wish I knew, Asmir,' she replied.

'When will Muris come?'

Aunt Melita ran her fingers through his hair. 'I don't know,' she said. And for a moment the light went out of her and she looked almost as old as Grandmother.

Asmir felt the tiny flame of hope within him flicker and waver. If Aunt Melita didn't know the answer . . . Then through the open window he heard the big bell and his heart grew steady again.

It took three evenings to do all the windows. And when they were finished there was not a pigeon dropping or a rain spot or a dust smudge to be seen. Asmir felt proud.

On Saturday morning they all packed up their things again. He was sorry to leave the big airy rooms and the chandeliers that glinted like a cloud of fireflies at night. He would miss the swans and the kangaroos and koalas. And the lady with the watching eyes. And most of all he would miss the sound of *Steffl*'s bell. The thought of getting to know yet another place, only to leave it again, made him feel hollow inside.

They stacked their luggage by the door and looked back. The apartment was gleaming clean to welcome Chris and his parents home. The only signs that they had been there at all were on the dining table – a bottle of wine, a new plant with a waxy red flower, and a drawing from Asmir on which he had printed THANK YOU.

# 11   A Ride To Remember

Then it was time to move out to Matthias's apartment. With George's help it didn't take long to carry the luggage downstairs.

Uncle Miroslav and Aunt Melita decided they wouldn't even try to fit everybody and everything into the car in one trip. So they took Grandmother and some cases first. Matthias led the way in his car with Vesna and George and more bags.

Asmir asked his mother if they could go to *Stephansplatz* to see the horses for the last time. They wouldn't be able to walk there from Matthias's. It was too far away.

As they reached the *Platz*, Asmir saw his favourite horses standing at the head of the line. He dragged Mirsada and Eldar to look at them. They were just as splendid as he remembered – as if they had come straight out of a picture book.

As they stood and watched the driver polishing the seats, a lady with pretty hair and a happy smile came up and talked to him. She was hiring the carriage for a drive. She climbed in. Asmir longed to be climbing up the steps to sit beside her.

She looked down and noticed Asmir and Eldar and their mother, and smiled and beckoned to them. 'Would you like to come with me?' she asked. 'It's not much fun going alone. It would be more fun with you.'

Asmir knew she was inviting them. He knew she was speaking English because their mother replied. Mirsada couldn't speak German yet, but she was now speaking English a little. Asmir could hardly wait for her nod before he was scrambling up, seating himself beside the kind stranger.

'Thank you,' he said. 'My name is Asmir. I am seven years old. My brother's name is Eldar. He is one and a half.' Then he added another new sentence. 'Our father, Muris, is in Sarajevo.'

The driver flicked the reins. The horses started up and the black spots rippled on their satin rumps. Eldar crowed and chortled. And even their mother's eyes were not sad. Asmir waved to the people in the street. And the lady took their photos. Asmir felt happy happy happy. He wished the drive would never end.

But it did. And then the lady took from her bag two little pins which she stuck through their T-shirts – a koala for Eldar and a kangaroo for Asmir. She patted their heads and squeezed their mother's hands.

'God bless you all,' she said. And she gave their mother a little card with writing on it. 'That's my address in Australia, if you should ever decide to come. Many people from your country have settled there. It's peaceful. It would be a good place for your boys to grow up.'

Asmir said, 'Thank you,' again and they waved her goodbye. He was sorry to see her go, even more sorry when his mother told him what she had said. He would love to go to Australia to see kangaroos and cuddle a koala. But it was so far away. How would Muris ever find them there?

# 12 'Was ist das?'

Matthias was waiting for them at the apartment. He took the key from their mother to give to Chris, and helped them into his car. It was time for them to move on again to the third place since they'd left home on that nightmare morning three months ago. Asmir shut out the unwanted memories of Sarajevo. Except for Muris. Was he still at home? Or had he gone to live with his mother and look after her?

Matthias's wife had taken their children to visit her parents and Matthias had moved to his sister's, so that they could have the apartment. It was not so large as Chris's, but it was more homely and cosy, with carpets and long velvet curtains and comfy armchairs. There was a separate little granny flat as well, for Vesna and George. And there were lots of toys. Asmir was glad that Matthias's children were girls. There were no guns.

There was a TV too and that night when Mirsada said, 'Time for bed,' Asmir would not go until he had watched the late news. He had missed it so much over the last three weeks. They all had. Perhaps they would see Muris. There were pictures of rockets exploding, setting fire to buildings. There were more pictures of more refugees in trains and in camps.

Asmir looked at them huddled in tents in the heat and felt very grateful to Chris and Matthias. Muris had taken them on a camping holiday once. But these tents and camps looked very different.

'Where will we go when we have to leave here?' he asked.

Nobody answered.

'Will we go to a camp like that?'

Aunt Melita hugged him. 'No. We won't have to go to a refugee camp.'

Asmir said, 'Will we go to Australia?'

'Australia? That's a long way away,' Aunt Melita said. 'Don't worry. We'll find somewhere right here, in Austria. In Vienna.'

'Where Muris can find us?'

'Of course,' Aunt Melita said.

He looked at Mirsada. He could see that his mother wanted to believe it too.

Asmir crept into the bed belonging to Matthias's elder daughter. He would do a thank-you picture for Matthias's family too.

Eldar was already fast asleep in the cot a metre away. Asmir almost envied his little brother. It was all right for him. He didn't watch TV at night and see the pictures and hear the sounds which brought back memories and stirred up fears Asmir didn't ever want to put into words. Eldar thought he had three mothers and an Uncle-Miroslav daddy as well as a Muris-photo daddy. He still thought everyone was his friend. No wonder he was so smiling and happy.

Asmir stretched and wriggled. It was the first time he'd slept in a bed by himself since they'd left Sarajevo. It was good to be able to stretch and wriggle, to have room and not to worry about disturbing someone else. But suddenly it seemed lonely too. Very lonely. He curled up into a little ball, remembering the last night in Sarajevo when he had slept in his father's arms.

'Oh, Muris,' he sobbed. And suddenly the tears he'd held back for so long came gushing out. Like the water escaping from a bombed main they'd seen in Sarajevo that night on TV.

Next night Chris invited them to meet his parents. It was fun to go back to the apartment. Asmir and Eldar felt very much at home in the big room with the firefly lights and the piano and the rocking chair.

Asmir looked at all the pictures again and knew the dark-eyed lady was watching as they all sat round eating the meal Chris and his mother had cooked. With candles on the table and a big bowl of cherries it was like a party. If only Muris were there . . .

George spoke English all evening with Chris and his parents, and translated everything for Vesna, his mother. Asmir wished that he had more English so that he could talk with them too. He would have to learn as fast as he could.

Monday was a busy day. George went off to work to clean cars with Uncle Miroslav as Chris had arranged. Asmir went with his mother to find the shops while Grandmother looked after Eldar. And Aunt Melita and Vesna went with Matthias to get their papers fixed, because he was an Austrian citizen and knew the laws.

Asmir had heard the grown-ups talking about it. He didn't properly understand, but he did know it was very important and they were all anxious about it.

They came home smiling, with a handful of cards officially stamped and signed. 'These are very precious. Now we are allowed to stay here. The Austrian Government has given us permits because Matthias has sponsored us. It is very good of him to say he will be responsible for us.'

'So now we are real refugees,' Asmir said.

'Yes,' said Aunt Melita. 'But we're luckier than most.'

On TV a few days later they saw just how lucky they were. The independent states of Slovenia and Croatia closed their borders and trainloads of refugees were stranded. Not able to get out, go back, go on or go home.

For two days the trains were not allowed to move and the people had to stay on board, all crowded together in the heat, without food or water. Asmir could hardly bear to watch. But he couldn't bear not to watch either. Neither could Mirsada. Suppose Muris was on one of those trains?

Then at last the trains were allowed to proceed and cross the border into the sanctuary which Austria was still giving. There were pictures of Austrian people waiting at the stations as the trains passed through, handing food and drinks and clothes and flowers up into the carriages. Asmir felt the tears pricking his eyes and a hot lump thick in his throat.

He hugged Uncle Miroslav. 'Thank you for being so brave.' And he hugged Aunt Melita. 'Thank you for looking after us.'

But that night the bad dreams came again.

And in the dreams Uncle Miroslav and Aunt Melita were not there to help.

Next week his mother Mirsada and Aunt Melita and Uncle Miroslav were starting German lessons in the evening. 'Can I come too?' he asked.

'This is for grown-ups,' Aunt Melita said. 'You'll learn when you go to school.'

'Can't I start with you?' Asmir begged his mother.

'We'll take you this time then,' she said. 'But we'll have to see what the teacher says.'

Asmir liked the teacher. She was cheerful and friendly. And it was exciting learning the names of things they used and saw every day, and finding out about things they didn't know.

'*Was ist das?*' Asmir learned to say. And he liked it. 'What is that?'

At the end of the lesson the teacher told Mirsada he could come every time if he wanted to. Asmir was thrilled. '*Was ist das?*' he kept saying all the way home.

Next day he told Eldar and Grandmother the words for table and chair, cup and spoon, knife and fork, milk and coffee and bread and cheese. When he went shopping with his mother he looked at all the words on the signs and found some that he had learned.

People at Chris's office asked Vesna to help

with their housecleaning. Vesna had had someone cleaning her house in Sarajevo. Now she tied
back her elegant hair, put on her plainest clothes
and went out to scrub other peoples' floors.
Matthias's parents asked her and Uncle Miroslav
to help them pack and unpack while they moved
house. Asmir wished he could get a job and earn
some money too.

Aunt Melita said, 'You are helping. You help
carry home the shopping every day. You teach
Grandmother and Eldar German.' And she gave
him some pocket money to spend just how he
liked.

The first week Asmir bought some new Lego
and he was very pleased. But the next week when
Aunt Melita asked what he planned to buy, he
said, 'I'm saving it for Muris. Father will need
some money too, when he comes.'

His mother hugged him. So did Aunt Melita.
But she didn't seem to be quite her usual self.
All weekend she seemed as if she expected the
phone to ring. But it never did. Was she waiting
for another call from Sarajevo? Asmir wondered.
Was there going to be news of Muris again soon?

On Sunday night he sat by the TV, switching
it from channel to channel, looking for news
from Sarajevo. It was all the same. More rockets,
more shells, more bombs, more tanks, more
snipers. Scenes in the hospitals. People queueing

in the streets for water. More people dead. More refugees. But no glimpse of his father.

'Time for bed,' Mirsada said. Her face was pale and drawn and there were inky smudges in the hollows beneath her eyes. But Asmir didn't want to go. He had the feeling something was going to happen. Aunt Melita still seemed to be listening for something. Somebody? Muris? Was Muris coming?

Then there was a ring at the door.

## 13  Milan's Escape

'Who can this be so late?' Grandmother said, and looked anxious.

Aunt Melita opened the door. Chris and Matthias were standing there. 'We've brought some people to see you,' Chris said.

A man stepped forward from behind them with an older lady. Asmir recognised Milan, George's father, from his two photos. Vesna ran to her husband. George put his arms round his grandmother. Vesna was crying. George was crying. Asmir was crying too. He was glad George had his father again. So glad. So glad too for George that he didn't have to look after his mother all by himself any more. But if only Chris could have brought Muris too . . . Asmir felt sick with disappointment.

Everyone was hugging everyone else. George's father picked up Asmir and gave him a special hug. George's grandmother hugged him too.

Vesna was hugging Chris. George was hugging Matthias.

Asmir hugged his mother. And she held him tight. She was smiling because all the others were so happy. But Asmir knew that the longing in her for Muris hurt more than any words could tell. Because he was hurting like that too.

They laughed, talked, drank, ate and listened, living every moment as Milan described how he had escaped from Sarajevo and Bosnia across Croatia and up the coast by boat. 'How did you manage it?' Uncle Miroslav wanted to know.

Milan told them. 'I left Sarajevo on Friday morning by a bus which went almost to Croatia. I got out before the terminus and walked into the village near the border. I found a man in a cafe who said he was willing to take me to a place where I could cross through the woods. But he said it would be better to wait until it was dark.'

Asmir shivered and took his mother's hand. George could not take his eyes off his father. Asmir knew George was seeing a hero and he felt jealous though he tried not to. He knew he would be like George if only it had been Muris.

Milan went on. 'The fellow wanted to be paid straightaway and as I parted with my money and handed over my luggage, I must say I wondered if he would keep his word. But I had to trust him. There was no other way.

'I got out of the village as quick as I could and hid at the edge of the wood. It was a long hot day, and I lay in the shade waiting and wondering. I was thinking about you, Vesna, of course, and you, George.'

Asmir could just imagine how Muris would be thinking of Mirsada – his precious Dada – and his Eldar and Asmir. He squeezed his mother's hand.

Milan continued. 'And I was thinking about you, Mother.' He smiled at her as she sat on Matthias's sofa, still dazed from the fear-filled journey. 'I was going to collect her in Split, I hoped,' he explained to the others. 'I was wondering whether ferries were still running up the coast from Split to Rijeka. The biggest worry was whether we would be able to get aboard.

'Chris had been keeping in touch through a contact in Rijeka. And he had promised to drive down to Croatia from Austria to collect us.'

Asmir looked at Chris. He was tall and dark too, like Muris. Would Chris drive to Croatia for Muris?

Milan went on. 'I was worrying whether Chris would get through to Rijeka. Or would the border be closed? Even if Chris did get through, would we be allowed out?

'And if we were allowed out, would we be allowed into Austria?'

Everybody in the room looked at each other. They all knew that feeling. Asmir saw Aunt Melita give Uncle Miroslav a special look. It was the sort of look Muris and Dada exchanged sometimes, especially if they thought no one was watching.

Milan took a gulp of coffee, as if the next bit was too hard to say. 'I must have patted the pocket which had my passport, papers and money a hundred times. And I ached inside for all that I knew and loved, realising that I probably would never see it again.' There was silence and Asmir could see tears creeping down his grandmother's cheeks. He snuggled up to her.

Milan continued. 'I watched the sun blazing across the sky and the shadows creeping out from the trees across the fields. The smell of the hay in the fields was so good after the stink of war.'

Asmir knew in his nostrils again the smell of Sarajevo burning. He could see again the grey smoke shroud and hear the pounding of the mortars. Muris was still breathing that smell day and night, and hearing that sound.

'And I listened to the larks and watched them like pinpoints against the blue sky.' Muris wouldn't be seeing skylarks or hearing them either.

'I sipped my water slowly to help a slice of bread go down. I listened to the crickets and

heard an owl call. A pair of bats darted overhead and the stars began to come out.' Milan paused again and they all waited.

'Then at last I heard a footfall. A dark shape was skirting along the edge of the fields. Twigs were cracking as it came.'

Asmir felt goose bumps coming up all over.

'I stood up quietly,' Milan said. 'A man called in a low voice. It was my man. I followed him.'

Asmir looked at George. George was watching his father and his hands were clenched.

'Branches brushed our arms, spiders' webs touched our faces. On and on in the dark we went. At last the man stopped. We had come to a faint pathway. He pointed the way I should go, shook my hand and wished me luck. And he was gone.

'I followed the trees until they began thinning. Then I curled up against a log and went to sleep. When I woke the sky was palest pink.'

Asmir thought of the soft glow from the lamp with the pink silk shade at home in Sarajevo.

'I could see the path to the village where the man was to meet me in his car with the luggage. Would he be there? I wondered.'

Everyone was holding their breath.

'I just had to believe he would be. Surely he would be.'

Asmir knew what Milan meant.

Milan smiled for the first time since he had begun his story. 'And he was. We had coffee and bread together, and he took me and my luggage to the bus which was going to Split. But now Split with its big harbour, a beautiful old town, has been damaged too by the fighting.' Milan shook his head sadly. 'Nothing is safe or sacred in war.'

And Asmir thought again of Muris's words, 'War never does make sense.'

Milan went on. 'My friend met me and we went to the house where Mother had been staying for months. It was so good to see her.' He patted her hand. 'We hurried to the wharf. Some ferries were still going up the coast, but they were crowded with people wanting to escape.'

Asmir remembered how they had had to run to catch the bus in Sarajevo, and the people all wanting to get on it. He felt choked by the panic and anxiety of it all again.

'We waited in the long queue, hoping we would get aboard. At last we got to the ticket counter and I bought the precious tickets.' He paused a moment, his face relaxing as he recalled the relief of that moment. 'Then it was pushing and shoving and jostling to climb the gangway with our luggage.

'I found a corner for Mother and stacked our stuff around her. There were piles of bags and bundles everywhere and people stretched out on the decks. It was another night under the stars, and a pretty uncomfortable one. I couldn't sleep for wondering if we would be turned back at one of the borders. And of course I was wondering if Chris had been able to get through.'

Asmir could see the agony and suspense showing on Milan's face again. And Uncle Miroslav was twisting his silver beard. Asmir remembered how white his knuckles had been as he gripped the steering wheel on their long journey.

'The early-morning sky promised more heat. But as the ship pulled in beside the wharf at last, I started to feel more hopeful,' Milan said. 'It was a slow business getting ashore. Everyone was eager and impatient. But finally we were on the wharf.

'Then we had another struggle with our luggage to get to the cafe where I had arranged to meet Chris, wondering at every step whether he would be there. But he was.'

Everyone in Matthias's sitting room began to clap. Asmir looked at Chris, dark and smiling. Smiling the way Muris smiled. Muris . . . Asmir felt tears burning behind his eyes. But he must not let them come. This was a happy time for Milan and his family.

Milan beamed. 'It was like a miracle. Chris was

gripping my hand. Matthias was helping Mother. They carried the luggage across the parking place to a large gleaming car.' Milan swallowed hard at the memory and his eyes filled with tears. 'Chris had brought the biggest and best model of his company's cars to meet us, to carry us to safety.' He leaned over and gripped Chris's hand. 'Thank you, friend. Thank you.'

# 14　*Chris's Rescue*

Chris took up the story. 'I'd taken the big car to impress the border guards. And put my windsurfer on top to look as if we were on holidays.' Chris grinned.

Asmir loved Chris's grin. It made him think of the way Muris joked.

'But even with such a large car it was a job to fit in everything and everybody. And I remembered how Dad had always worked fitting everything in, packing and re-packing when we went on holidays in Australia.'

Asmir smiled gratefully at Uncle Miroslav. He'd worked so hard fitting all their luggage into his little car, never even suggesting that the rucksack of toys be left behind. And he remembered Muris helping everyone to stow all their stuff somehow on that bus in Sarajevo.

Chris continued. 'Matthias and I left Austria before daybreak, without even stopping for

93

breakfast. We drove all morning through Slovenia to Croatia to reach Rijeka. But we didn't know whether Milan and his mother would be on the ferry.

'After we picked them up I suggested having lunch along the way. But they did not want to stop. She was cold with shock, wrapped in a shawl and a rug, huddled in her corner, not speaking, not even smiling. Milan was silent too, tired and tense in his corner.'

Asmir remembered how cold he had suddenly felt in that plane. How even with Mirsada's arms around him and Eldar between his knees he was cold. Cold in every part of him. Cold with knowing they were going. Going away from all that he had always known. The chill ran through him again with clammy fingers, bringing him up in goose flesh all over. Freezing the last picture of Muris, being grabbed by the soldiers, in an icy frame in his head. He shivered and snuggled up to his mother as Chris went on.

'It was hot and the car was frying hot too. But each time we turned on the air conditioner Milan and his mother began to shiver. So we drove on and on, hungry, thirsty and sweltering.'

Asmir remembered the long hot car journey across Hungary, that had seemed as if it would never end.

Chris said, 'Matthias and I had worked out

our plans for the border crossings. The car has Austrian registration with a Viennese number plate. Matthias has an Austrian passport with a Viennese address, so we decided he should be the driver at the crossings.

'He would hand in the passports with his on top, mine underneath and then Milan's. At the bottom of the pile we put Milan's mother's because it wasn't valid any more.'

Everyone in the room was silent, tense with memories of border checkpoints. Asmir noticed Uncle Miroslav's hands were clenched and he could see tears glinting behind Aunt Melita's glasses. Grandmother seemed to have stopped breathing. Mirsada was holding his hand so tightly it hurt.

'As we approached the Slovenian border Matthias took over the wheel. The silence in the car became heavier. It became so heavy I was glad we had the most powerful engine to cope.' Chris was making a joke of it now. But Asmir could remember that silence. Like a great weight pressing on his chest so that he could hardly breathe, let alone even whisper.

Chris continued. 'We passed through the Croatian side without being stopped. At the Slovenian checkpoint the guard looked at the Austrian number plate, then up at the wind-surfer and waved us through. Matthias and I smiled. But there were still no smiles from the back.'

Asmir looked at Milan. His face was stretched tight, paper white with pain. His mother was holding her shawl up to her face.

Chris went on. 'We changed places again and drove on, tired and hungry, sucking peppermints. I turned on the radio so Milan could listen to the news. We were certainly relieved when he said there was no report of borders being closed. But we knew it didn't guarantee free exit. They could still be closed without warning.

'I was watching our precious passengers in the rear vision mirror. Their faces were more drawn every moment, more numb with every kilometre.'

George and Vesna were staring at Milan. Chris said, 'I thought of the families in Vienna, wondering, worrying. It would be worst for Melita, because she was the only one I'd let into the secret of the rescue plan. It would've been cruel to raise hopes in Vesna and George, in case something went wrong.'

Chris was kind, Asmir thought. Kind like Muris. And Miroslav. He looked at his uncle looking at Aunt Melita. She smiled up at him and squeezed his hand. Asmir swallowed hard and squeezed Dada's hand.

Chris was saying, 'Then it was time to change places again. In the car it was stifling with heat and fear. Slowing down was agony. I longed for Matthias to put his foot on the accelerator and drive through both checkpoints. But of course he didn't.' Chris grinned. Asmir knew that wild longing.

'We held our breath as we came to the Slovenian crossing.' Everyone in the room held their breath.

'For the second time the Austrian number-plate *and* the windsurfer got us through without a glance at the passports.' Chris grinned again.

Then he was serious once more. 'But it was different at the Austrian checkpoint.

'There the car was stopped.

'The guard barely looked at Matthias's passport, and just flicked through mine. But when he came to Milan's he bent down and looked into the car. Matthias and I had planned what to say if there was any trouble and how we would argue for Milan and his mother to be allowed into Austria. Matthias is good at winning arguments.' Chris flashed a smile at his friend and workmate.

'But it wasn't necessary. The guard looked at the bottom passport, twelve years out of date. He looked at Milan's mother huddled with her lap full of bundles. "Welcome," he said and handed back the passports.

'So we drove into Austria.'

Everyone let out a sigh. Asmir saw Uncle Miroslav's shoulders relax.

'I turned and gripped Milan's hand. It was a moment I'll never forget,' Chris said quietly. 'Milan had tears in his eyes and his mother was sobbing into her shawl. Even then they did not want to stop. The border was a hundred kilometres behind before they finally agreed.'

Asmir swallowed. It felt as if there was an orange stuck in his throat. Oh Muris, he sobbed. But not a sound came out.

Chris said, 'We found a restaurant terrace overlooking a lake, with tables under yellow umbrellas, and tubs of red geraniums – just the right place to celebrate. Milan's mother stared at the menu. After the food shortages of war, all the pages of choices in a foreign language were too much.

'So I ordered the biggest platter of cheese and ham, sausage and hard-boiled eggs while we waited for a typical Austrian meal – Wiener schnitzels with chips and salad.'

Asmir could just taste that schnitzel in its golden crumbs and those chips crisp outside, moist inside. How Muris would enjoy a meal like that!

Chris said, 'I'll never forget what Milan said as he took his third egg, "In Sarajevo an egg costs ten times as much as a bullet. And for every egg there are a hundred bullets."'

Asmir thought of Muris among the bullets. How long since he had had an egg? And when would he be able to escape? He looked at his mother and knew what she was thinking. He said to Aunt Melita, 'Will Chris drive to Rijeka to fetch Muris when he comes with his mother?'

'Of course,' Chris said, lifting him on to his knee. Chris still smelled faintly of aftershave, although the shadow of tomorrow's whiskers was dark around his chin. Asmir could feel the slight prickle of his cheek as Chris bent over him. Just like Muris.

Asmir yawned, and yawned again. Somehow his eyelids wouldn't stay open, although he still had another question. 'Can I come too?' he wanted to ask. But he was asleep before he could say it.

Chris had carried him to bed and tucked him in. And Asmir had dreamed of Muris. Muris coming. Coming through the door.

Then the dream had changed. Changed to a nightmare. Soldiers with guns . . . grabbing Muris . . . taking him away . . . Muris behind barbed wire . . . Muris gaunt and grim and grey . . . And graves . . . holes and humps where he used to roll on green grass with his playmates . . . and flames he could neither fight nor flee . . . fierce hungry flames . . . burning burning burning all that was familiar . . .

He woke sweating and trembling in his mother's arms. She cradled him and crooned to him, rocking him as if he were Eldar. Lucky Eldar who didn't have a hundred hundred memories. Heavy horrible memories he didn't want. Memories he tried to push down and shut out. Memories which came seeping in through whatever he was thinking. Creeping in through the chinks in his courage in the daylight. Sweeping in like a flood at night through his sleep. Fears and feelings without words. Tears and terrors he couldn't tell.

'Do you have bad dreams too?' he whispered to his mother. And he felt her soft hair brush his cheek as she nodded. They shared their pain in a long close silence that wrapped them round like a blanket.

Then she spoke. 'But always remember, Asmir, that whatever happens . . .' There was a catch in her voice and Asmir shivered and burrowed even closer into her sweet warmth.

She began again. 'Whatever happens,' she said strongly. 'Muris is always alive in our hearts.'

Suddenly the little candle of hope seemed as if it would never gutter and die. And Asmir didn't envy Eldar any longer. Eldar had some memories of Muris, but he, Asmir, had far more. Good, happy, proud memories he would share with his little brother.

# 15  A Present From Muris

Asmir was proud of his mother. Mirsada was so brave and strong. She never said how much she missed Muris. But Asmir knew how sore her heart really was. She had taken charge of the housekeeping. Now with ten people in the apartment there was always cleaning and washing, shopping and cooking to do. But every moment she could spare she used for German study.

She said, 'I must learn German as soon as I can. I want to be able to read and write it properly, as well as speaking it, so that I can get a job. And so I can teach Muris when he comes.'

She watched the TV advertisements very carefully and looked at all the pamphlets and free newspapers that were stuffed into the letter box. She wrote out the shopping list each day in German and tried to read all the signs in the supermarket as well as the labels on the packets and cans and bottles.

Asmir enjoyed doing it too and always sat at the table helping her with the homework for the German class, or drawing. He liked drawing pictures for some of the words they were learning.

She was getting on much faster than Aunt Melita and Uncle Miroslav. They often fell asleep during the lesson. It was so hot in the classroom and they had both been up since five o'clock with a long day at work. On the days they went to class Asmir had a nap with Eldar in the afternoon. He didn't want anyone to say that he couldn't come because he should be home in bed.

On the other afternoons Asmir and his mother would go out while Grandmother and Eldar were having a nap. They would go to a museum or gallery if it was a free day. Or they would go to the Imperial Palace and look at the statues, the horses and carriages, the fountains and the pigeons. Or they would wander along the streets where the finest shops were – *Kaerntnerstrasse*, *Kohlmarkt* and the *Graben* – looking in the windows.

'After all, it doesn't cost anything to look,' his mother would say.

Their favourites were the special chocolate

shops. They would stand in front of the windows gazing at all the wonderful things. Cars, cigars, balls, bottles, even brown striped ties nestling on white shirt fronts, all made of chocolate. Fans, hearts and roses too. And beautiful boxes with pretty painted pictures on their lids, and satin and lace and shining ribbons, red and royal blue, gold and silver.

'It's a feast for the eyes,' his mother would smile. But he always heard the little sigh under her breath.

Then he had an idea which he kept secret. He didn't even tell Aunt Melita. But he spoke to the teacher at German class and asked her to help him.

One day he counted up all the money he had saved. It was enough for a whole pack of Lego. He put it carefully in his pocket without saying anything to anyone. And when they went off exploring he steered his mother in the direction of the best chocolate shop of all.

But instead of standing outside in front of the window, he walked in, holding Mirsada firmly by the hand. It was very beautiful inside, with chandeliers and little gilt chairs.

'Asmir,' she said, trying to pull him back outside. 'We've only come to look.'

'Not today, Dada,' Asmir said. He walked up

to the counter. 'Sit down,' he said to her. 'It's a surprise.'

Then he said to the assistant. 'I would like a rose bud, please. The smallest one, in the prettiest box tied with red ribbon.'

And he began counting out Muris's money, the money he had been saving for him.

The assistant chose a bud and laid it in its little box. She tied it up with red ribbon and handed it to Asmir.

He gave it to his mother. 'Dada, this is from Muris.'

He turned to the assistant and explained in the sentences he had been practising for weeks, 'We come from Sarajevo. Muris is my father. He is still there. My mother was the chemical engineer in the chocolate factory. It was bombed. When she has learnt German better she hopes to find work in Vienna.' He bowed to her as he had seen Matthias bow to Grandmother.

She looked at the grave-faced lady with the sad brown eyes, still sitting on the little gilt chair, holding the tiny box with its precious gift. She said, 'You have learnt German very well. I am glad you like our shop. You are welcome to come in and look as often as you wish.'

Asmir bowed again and escorted his mother from the shop.

Outside she found her voice. 'Thank you, Asmir.' She kissed him and smiled. And for a moment she looked like the mother he remembered in Sarajevo. 'It's the most beautiful present I've ever been given.'

## 16  Settled

That weekend they went for a picnic to a lake where Chris had once taken Milan windsurfing. It was lovely to run on the grass and paddle in the water and sit under the shady trees.

But Asmir was shocked when Milan said, 'If the war goes on, there won't be a tree left in Sarajevo by the end of the winter. They'll all have been cut down for firewood.' And Asmir thought of the trees he used to climb in the playground.

The next Saturday Chris showed them another place along the River *Donau* where there was a pebbly beach. Eldar loved the water and cried every time they tried to get him out. And they all enjoyed it so much they went back again on Sunday.

But Asmir couldn't forget the refugees in camps.

'Where are we going to live when Matthias comes back?' he asked Aunt Melita again.

'I don't know yet,' she said. 'But Chris is helping me to look for an apartment of our own. We're going every day at lunchtime. It's hard because so many people want apartments. But we'll find something. Don't you worry.'

It wasn't easy. There were so many people hunting for them that places had often been let by the time they got there. And some landlords didn't want refugees. For the sake of Grandmother and Mirsada, Aunt Melita tried not to show how tired and discouraged she felt. But Asmir knew.

Then one night she came home excited. They'd seen two places. One was close and cheap. But it was shabby and needed doing up and the landlord was not very friendly. The other was further away near a lovely big park. It was freshly painted and had a kindly landlord. But it cost more.

Next evening she took Uncle Miroslav to see them. At the first one the landlord didn't turn up. And when they got to the second the nice landlord was waiting, but there was a blackout, so Miroslav could only see it by torchlight.

It was more expensive than they could afford, but it had two bedrooms. Asmir heard the grown-ups discussing it. Uncle Miroslav was worried about the cost. Very worried. But next morning it was decided. They would take it.

Asmir felt so glad. He hugged Aunt Melita and Uncle Miroslav. 'Are George and Vesna and Milan and his mother coming with us too?'

'No,' Aunt Melita said. 'Matthias's brother is lending them his holiday cottage. It's an hour's drive from Vienna. But we can still have picnics together.'

Uncle Miroslav and Aunt Melita moved first to get the apartment ready. Chris gave them cups and plates, knives, forks and spoons, a saucepan and some chairs he didn't need. Matthias offered a sofa. A lady at Aunt Melita's office gave sheets and towels from her linen cupboard and blankets too. Aunt Melita bought an iron, a clothes horse and some pillows.

It was a double celebration because it was Uncle Miroslav's birthday too. While he and Aunt Melita were shopping and arranging everything in their new home, Mother and Grandmother were preparing the birthday dinner. And Asmir was making the birthday card. Uncle Miroslav and Aunt Melita told them all about the new apartment over dinner, then went off to sleep there.

It seemed strange without them. Lonely. That night he had the running away dream again. And again. The first time he slipped and fell. In a pool of blood. The second time the suitcase burst open, scattering all their precious things. And there was no one to help.

Then it was another week of cleaning and polishing to leave Matthias's apartment as fresh and sparkling as they could make it. Asmir put all the toys back tidily in the big basket, stacked the books on the shelves and did a thank-you drawing for the little girls. He and Eldar had had so much fun with all their things. They would miss them.

He repacked their own toys for the fourth time and repacked their clothes. He was glad this would be the last time. And he hoped the dreams wouldn't come with him.

In the new apartment he unpacked everything carefully in the bedroom where Grandmother would sleep and where he and Eldar would play. Inside and on top of a big carton he arranged their teddies, his Lego, Eldar's horse and cart, their books, the panda and the puppy, the stacking rings and tinkly ball, his coloured pencils and drawing pad.

But Eldar liked the carton better for playing houses and boats and cars. It didn't matter. He could arrange them all again before Grandmother went to bed.

There was no TV. So Asmir put up the photos of Muris. One in the living room by the sofa where they would sleep. The other by the kitchen table so that Muris would be there while they ate.

There was no telephone either.

'How will Muris ring us?'

'His friend will ring me at the office, like he did before,' Aunt Melita said. Before. It was weeks ago. Weeks and weeks and weeks ago. Neither of them said how many.

As he curled up that night on the sofa Asmir heard a clock striking. He wished he could still hear *Steffl*'s deep bell which had greeted him on the first morning in Vienna. It was too far away. Not as far as Muris. But too far to hear.

But there was a big chestnut tree outside the window and its leaves were rustling in the breeze. He thought of the chestnut trees in Sarajevo and their tall candles of blossoms which the bees loved. And he fell asleep and dreamed that he was home with his father.

On Sunday as they ate breakfast together for the first time in their own apartment, they could hear another bell ringing. Not so deep as *Steffl*, but clear and calm and comforting. Asmir knew that God was still listening. And felt safe.

On Monday he and his mother went exploring. They followed the smell of fresh bread and found the baker. Then they found the

supermarket and the shoe repair shop. They found the stop for the tram that would take them back into the city. And they found the school. It didn't look very different from schools in Sarajevo. Asmir looked forward to being with other children again after nearly six months. It would be fun.

As they walked home along under the chestnut trees Mirsada said, 'I'm going to miss your help with the shopping when you go to school.'

Asmir looked up at the clusters of spiky green chestnuts. By the time they split open and the shiny brown nuts came tumbling down, he would have walked along here many times, his school bag on his back.

He would have new friends. He would be playing new games. He would be speaking German every day. He would have learned all sorts of new things.

He wanted to learn as much as he could as fast as he could, so that he could look after his mother and Eldar and Grandmother, and help Aunt Melita and Uncle Miroslav. He wanted Muris to be proud of him.

And when he grew up he would be a lawyer like his father. Or an engineer like his mother. Or a teacher perhaps. Or an architect planning beautiful new buildings for Sarajevo. Or he might be an artist doing pictures of pigeons and horses and roses and dogs on chocolate boxes for special presents.

But one thing he knew he never would be. He would never be a soldier.

## About the Story

*No Gun For Asmir* was inspired by the courage of two Bosnian refugee families I got to know in June 1992 – Melita's and Milan's. We were visiting our son Chris in Vienna. His work as public affairs manager for one of Europe's biggest car manufacturers covers all Eastern and Central Europe and he was very concerned for the safety of the journalists he employed in the country that had been Yugoslavia.

Melita's family is of Muslim background. She and her Serbian husband Miroslav had left Sarajevo, the capital of Bosnia Herzegovina, earlier. Miroslav was also a journalist, working for the main Yugoslav news service. They had foreseen the troubles which would follow the break-up of Yugoslavia, as the various states claimed their independence. They settled in Belgrade, the capital city of Yugoslavia and of the state of Serbia.

Croatia and Slovenia both declared themselves sovereign states and were attacked by the Serbian-led former Yugoslav army. Historic towns were shelled and beautiful old buildings destroyed. Innocent civilians, men, women and children were killed or driven from their homes.

When Bosnia Herzegovina declared its independence in March 1992, Melita became very worried for her mother and sister Mirsada in Sarajevo, and Mirsada's husband Muris and their two little boys, Asmir and Eldar. Bosnia Herzegovina has had a Muslim majority for over four hundred years since it was overrun by the Turks, made part of the Ottoman empire and its Slavic people converted to Islam. Now the new Serbian invaders wanted to dispossess the Muslim population. And all Melita's family were Muslim. Their very lives were in danger.

Milan is Serbian. His wife Vesna's father had been a general in the Serbian army. Milan is also a journalist and had a good job in Sarajevo. Vesna ran a fashion boutique, and together they had set up a successful restaurant. But they saw their life savings and years of hard work vanish when the restaurant was destroyed and its stores looted in the early days of the war.

Milan loved Sarajevo and its people. He wanted to live in peace with his Muslim friends, neighbours and workmates. But the war was filling people with fear and suspicion and distrust. It was no place for their son George to be growing up. He is a tall boy and at fourteen he could be forced into military service to fight against their Muslim friends. So while it was still possible to travel, Milan sent Vesna and George away from Sarajevo to Belgrade.

Not long afterwards Melita heard in Belgrade through her newspaper *Oslobodjenje*, which means liberation, that it would soon become impossible for civilians to leave Sarajevo. She phoned her sister Mirsada and told her, urging her to try to bring their mother and the children out on a mercy flight which was leaving that very day. By a superhuman effort Mirsada managed it. And it turned out to be the very last such plane allowed to leave Sarajevo.

But Muris, Asmir and Eldar's father, had to stay behind. Muslim men were not allowed to leave. He had an injury which exempted him from fighting, but he did not want to be rounded up and sent to a prison camp. He went into hiding.

I wrote the story in Austria between July and September 1992. The Austrian government was leading the world in giving sanctuary and help to the Bosnian refugees. The Austrian people were wholeheartedly supporting a community program, *Nachbar in Not, (Neighbour in Need)*, sending relief in to the war-stricken people of Bosnia. Every day there were new reports of the war in the papers and new pictures on TV of the plight of its victims.

At the time of writing this note (May 1993), Mirsada had just received a letter from Muris delivered by hand. It had been written in March and early April and was full of double meanings in case it was intercepted. He was longing for his family whom he hadn't seen for twelve months. Cousins of Melita and Mirsada had been imprisoned, tortured, shot. But money which Melita had managed to send through her network of contacts had reached him and other family members.

In Vienna, Asmir is enjoying school. Eldar is beginning to talk in both Serbo-Croatian and German. But Grandmother misses her family and friends, and is very lonely. Melita's salary has to support the whole family.

Both Miroslav and Mirsada have been looking for employment and have done an intensive German course. Miroslav's job at the garage lasted only a few months and all his efforts to obtain a work permit and find another job have been unsuccessful. He has now gone temporarily to Germany in the hope of finding seasonal farm work.

Mirsada, with Matthias's help, applied to twenty-one chocolate factories and was thrilled to receive a two-month contract at one of the biggest. Although it was not extended, she has now been offered re-employment with a work permit when the factory moves to a new site, an hour's travel from Vienna, in June.

Milan could not find regular employment or permanent housing. So although George had started school in Vienna and was doing well, the family decided to move to Norway, where the government is now offering more help for refugees. They left Vienna on Christmas Day.

Both families spent Christmas Eve together with Chris in his apartment, which had been their first home in Vienna.

We would gladly help both families come to Australia. But because we are not related, we are not eligible to sponsor them. And because they have no relatives here and their professional qualifications are not wanted, they are not eligible to emigrate in their own right.

*Christobel Mattingley*
*Stonyfell, South Australia*
*21 May 1993*

After many months campaigning by his family and supporters, including Australian, British and German publishers, Muris finally obtained permission in April 1994 to leave Sarajevo. He had an anxious journey of six days to Zagreb, where he spent several more weeks because of problems in obtaining an Austrian visa. After a temporary visa was issued he was reunited at the end of May in Vienna with his family whom he had not seen for almost 26 months.

Muris's main motives for surviving the terrible two years in Sarajevo were his family and the urge to tell the story of what ordinary civilians went through during the seige. I am now working on writing that story with his help.

*Christobel Mattingley*
*24 August 1994*
*Vienna*

## About the Author

'I was seven years old when the first rumblings of World War Two in Europe came crackling through the big wireless set in the corner of the sitting room of my first home at Brighton, South Australia. The stories of the early waves of refugees made me so anxious I packed my own special treasures in my kindergarten case and kept it ready under my bed.

'I have never been a refugee, but my father's work as an engineer brought our family three major interstate moves in Australia. The first came when I was just eight and we left that beloved home, school, playmates, pets and fond grandparents, aunts, uncles and cousins.

'My first job after graduating in 1951 from the University of Tasmania was helping displaced persons of Europe who were arriving in Australia as migrants. Since then I have lived in

Europe for short periods and know the feeling of being without language in someone else's country.'

Christobel Mattingley

*No Gun for Asmir* is Christobel's thirty-second book for children, and her second story about refugees. Her first was the much loved and widely acclaimed story of World War Two, *The Angel With a Mouth Organ*, published in 1984. Another major work focussing on the plight of dispossessed people was *Survival in Our Own Land*, which tells the story of the one hundred and fifty years of occupation of South Australia from the Aboriginal point of view.

Many of Christobel's books have been translated and some have been made into films for the ABC, or have won awards in Australia and the United States. In 1990, Christobel Mattingley received the Advance Australia Award for Service to Literature.

## About the Illustrator

Elizabeth Honey has illustrated many books,
including Christobel Mattingley's *Brave With
Ben*. She also wrote and illustrated *Princess
Beatrice and the Rotten Robber*, *The Cherry Dress*
and *Honey Sandwich* (an Honour Book in the
1994 Children's Book Council Book of the Year
Awards for Younger Readers).

Several years ago, Elizabeth and her husband
travelled through Tito's Yugoslavia. More
recently, Elizabeth and her family visited
Vienna, where they met Chris. Elizabeth's
interest in that part of the world, her friendship
with the Mattingleys, and the heart-rending
story of these sudden refugees made this a
special project for her.

Elizabeth lives in Richmond, Melbourne, with
her husband, her daughter, and her son who is
the same age as Asmir. *No Gun for Asmir* is
illustrated in 2B pencil.

# MORE GREAT READING FROM PUFFIN
☆☆☆☆☆☆☆☆☆☆☆☆☆☆☆☆☆☆☆☆☆☆☆☆☆☆☆☆☆

**The Sack**   Christobel Mattingley/Illustrated by Simon Kneebone

When Shane's dad loses his job, everything changes, slowly at first and then faster and faster. But although Shane and his family have to give up so much that is familiar, Shane finds that, in their new life, they still have what is most important.


**The Twenty-Seventh Annual African Hippopotamus Race**
Morris Lurie/Illustrated by Elizabeth Honey

Eight-year-old Edward trains very hard for this greatest of swimming marathons with no idea of the cunning and jealousy he'll meet from the other competitors. This best-selling story takes you behind the scenes and shows you just what it takes to become a champion.

*Winner of the Young Australians' Best Book Award (YABBA) 1986.*


**The Black Duck**   Eleanor Nilsson/Illustrated by Rae Dale

When Tom and his family move from their farm at Kangarilla, Tom has to leave his much loved pet behind – a little wild black duck called Squeak Toy. But, mistakenly, he thinks that Squeak Toy will be returned to him on his birthday, and when she isn't, he sets out to find her . . .

*Shortlisted for the 1991 Australian Children's Book of the Year Award for younger readers.*

# MORE GREAT READING FROM PUFFIN

☆☆☆☆☆☆☆☆☆☆☆☆☆☆☆☆☆☆☆☆☆☆☆☆☆

**Against the Odds**   Robin Klein/Illustrated by Bill Wood

Five improbable stories from a master storyteller. A nine-year-old girl rids a town of aliens, a genie brings more than magic to suburbia and a pocket-sized visitor gives the gift of confidence to a shy boy.

*Shortlisted for the 1989 NSW Premier's Literary Awards.*

**The Last Week in December**   Ursula Dubosarsky

Bonnie has a terrible, guilty secret, something she did three years ago when her English relatives were visiting. Now they are returning to Australia and Bonnie fears the worst . . .

**The Watching Lake**   Elaine Forrestal

Bryn and his family have moved near a lake. But bulldozers have disturbed the sinister Min Min slumbering in the misty waters. Years ago, the Min Min lured a woman to her death . . . This time it has chosen Bryn.

*Shortlisted for the 1991 WA Premier's Literary Award.*

# MORE GREAT READING FROM PUFFIN

☆☆☆☆☆☆☆☆☆☆☆☆☆☆☆☆☆☆☆☆☆☆☆☆☆☆☆☆☆

**The Nimbin**   Jenny Wagner

Philippa's summer holidays started off ordinarily enough until she was adopted by a little creature, a nimbin, who decided to make her beach bag its home, getting Philippa into all sorts of trouble.


**Return of the Nimbin**   Jenny Wagner

The sequel to the immensely popular story about Philippa and her friend the nimbin – the little creature with a bad temper and an enormous appetite.


**Old Sam, Jasper and Mr Frank**
Trevor Todd/Illustrated by Betty Greenhatch

Old Sam's one great interest in life is his chickens – he's certainly not interested in kids! But things begin to change when a pigeon finds its way into the shed and Sam's interest in it is shared with a young Aboriginal boy who moves in next door.

*Shortlisted for the 1985 South Australian Peace Literature Award.*

# MORE GREAT READING FROM PUFFIN

☆ ☆ ☆ ☆ ☆ ☆ ☆ ☆ ☆ ☆ ☆ ☆ ☆ ☆ ☆ ☆ ☆ ☆ ☆ ☆ ☆ ☆ ☆ ☆ ☆ ☆ ☆ ☆ ☆ ☆ ☆ ☆.☆ ☆

**Teacher's Secret**   Michael Dugan/Illustrated by Jacqui Young

In the summer of 1920, Evie is about to start a new school year as the only girl in the little Tintababbi school. But her new teacher is a surprise and the secret in the schoolhouse garden changes Evie's life forever.

**Not Again, Dad!**   Thurley Fowler/Illustrated by Craig Smith

Paul knew how to manage Mum, but when she's away and Dad becomes household manager, it isn't so easy. The worst part is when Dad joins in on cricket and swimming classes – totally embarrassing!

**The Return of The Baked Bean**   Debra Oswald

Swept along on a flooded river in a runaway caravan called The Baked Bean, Gina Terrific has to think fast to get herself out of some hair-raising and hilarious predicaments.

# MORE GREAT READING FROM PUFFIN

☆☆☆☆☆☆☆☆☆☆☆☆☆☆☆☆☆☆☆☆☆☆☆☆☆☆☆☆☆☆

**I Hate Fridays!**   Rachel Flynn/Illustrated by Craig Smith

A collection of stories about characters in the classroom, about all the funny, sad and traumatic things that can happen. Hilariously illustrated by the very popular Craig Smith.

*A Children's Book Council of Australia Notable Book, 1991.*


**It's Not Fair!**   Rachel Flynn/Illustrated by Craig Smith

More hilarious stories from the kids at Koala Hills Primary School. In this second book, following *I Hate Fridays*, you can discover more funny things about Kirsty, Sam and the others.


**I Can't Wait!**   Rachel Flynn/Illustrated by Craig Smith

It's the last year of primary school for the characters from Koala Hills. Thadeus can finally sit with Kirsty, but is it really what he wants after all? Kerrie's dream to ride a horse comes true, but is it what she imagined? Peter gets a girlfriend, but will he ever think of anything to say to her? Following the huge success of *I Hate Fridays!* and *It's Not Fair!*, here are your favourite characters back again in grade six.